OTHER BOOKS BY JANE SMILEY

Barn Blind
At Paradise Gate
Duplicate Keys

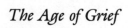

The Age of Grief

The Age of Grief

A NOVELLA
AND STORIES BY

JANE
SMILEY

Alfred A. Knopf

NEW YORK

1 9 8 7

Some stories in this work were originally published in the
following publications: The Atlantic, Mademoiselle,
and TriQuarterly.

"The Age of Grief" was originally published in The
Quarterly, Vol. I, Spring 1987. Copyright ©1987 by
Jane Smiley.

Library of Congress Cataloging-in-Publication Data

Smiley, Jane.
    The age of grief.

    I. Title.
PS3569.M39A7   1987   813'.54   87-45120.
ISBN 0-394-55848-0

Manufactured in the United States of America
FIRST EDITION

CONTENTS

The Age of Grief

The
Pleasure
of Her
Company

*W*hen Florence comes up the sidewalk toward her duplex, she can see that the large Victorian house just to the south has new owners. It is the one lovely place on her otherwise undistinguished block—porched, corniced, many-peaked, and recently painted Nordic blond with piqué white trim. Each of these last few evenings she has admired, as she does tonight, how neatly the trim glows in the twilight. She threads her way past boxes and pieces of furniture the owners have left on the sidewalk. There are two piles of women's clothing. Dishes and cutlery are stacked beside the curb, and a slender-legged plant stand supports two ferns and a grape ivy. A brown box, its lid agape, contains the *Oxford English Dictionary*, abridged edition, and two Mexican cookbooks. Draped over the back of a kitchen chair is a white dress, perhaps a wedding dress, its bodice shaped into fullness with blue tissue paper. One of its stiff lace cap sleeves has fallen off the hanger. As Florence notices this, a breeze lifts the skirt. She rearranges the sleeve on the hanger and, shy of being caught, hurries the rest of the way home. In the morning when she turns with her coffee cup to gaze out the window of her kitchen, the items are still on the lawn. The dress has fallen off the chair and lies spread on the green grass like a snow angel.

While she is at work, everything disappears, and that night, at last, there are lights in the windows; the stained glass she has coveted for years bejewels the darkness. There is more to covet, or at least envy, when she finally meets the Howards—Philip and Frannie. Two handmade orange rugs are flung on the hardwood floors and three or four large paintings, stretched but unframed, furnish the wide walls. There are plants. Mostly, however, there is space, so much pale floor that the rooms, as she looks through to the back porch, fit across one another like layers, inexhaustible, promising, culminating in sunlight.

Frannie has copper-colored eyes, winged brows, and short, springy hair that she obviously does no more to than wash into shape. She asks Florence to sit at the round maple table for tea. Everything about Frannie, from her clumsiness with the teacups to her delight with the muffins Florence has brought for housewarming, is inviting. There is a footstep, and Frannie glances up, then takes out another plate. "Hello!" says Philip, but before he sits down, he strides around the periphery of the room, stopping twice to admire the walls and floors, to look through the open door to the front porch, to smile and put his hands on his hips. Frannie says, "Philip still can't believe we own the place. Last night I found him out on the front porch holding on to the gingerbread and staring at the stained glass."

Philip sits at the table and leans toward Florence on his elbows. "Have you ever house-hunted? You wouldn't believe what some people do to their houses. I went to one place that looked rather charming from the outside, you know, but inside they'd cut doorways where they shouldn't have been and added on this room at the back, plastic paneling, spongy rug like fungus. It wasn't a bad house, at one time. I went outside and threw up in a trash barrel."

"Philip took house-hunting very seriously," says Frannie.

"You see how people live." He butters a muffin.

Philip, it turns out, was in high school with Florence's brother. Philip tells them that no two strangers in the nation are separated by more than five intermediate acquaintances. When he finds out that Florence is a nurse, he asks her if she saves a life every day, and when Frannie mentions her job, directing foreign exchange programs and charter flights for the local university, he says, "Importing exotica, exporting domestica." He obviously expects to fill air and space, and he is quite handsome, but it is Frannie that Florence can't help looking at. She sits smiling over the conversation like a child over a jack-in-the-box, waiting to be surprised into laughter. She makes Florence long to say something hilarious.

Florence goes next door, thinking that she really shouldn't be visiting again so soon. She has been there every day, sometimes twice, since they moved in two weeks ago. She brings a quarter pound of a new kind of tea, knowing that it is almost a bribe, and shouts a comical "YOO-hoo!" as she crosses the threshold. Frannie giggles from the side porch and responds in kind. The giggle is a tremendous relief to Florence, because she is ready to detect signs of boredom and exasperation in Frannie's first glance at her. The giggle allays her fears, and she grins as she pulls out a maple chair beside the maple table once again, investing the moment with her fullest, most tangible pleasure at being liked. Philip isn't there.

Florence talks about the hospital, where she is a nurse

in pediatrics. Already, Frannie has learned the names of the doctors, secretaries, and other nurses, and her evident interest renders Florence almost eloquent. She talks about the medical student she had been seeing (too young) and the photographer she is seeing now (too self-absorbed). She talks about recipes and being on the Pill and having gained and lost thirty pounds in four months. Frannie's questions and responses create such vivid images in her mind, and her smiles and rejoinders are so appropriate, that Florence grows ecstatic with conversation. She feels as though her words leap at Frannie before Frannie even finishes speaking. She follows Frannie around the house, talking. Frannie sweeps the floor, puts away the breakfast dishes, straightens one of the orange rugs, makes their bed. While Frannie is balling together Philip's socks, Florence sits on the floor of their bedroom talking and fitting the soles of Frannie's shoes along the soles of her feet. She is interested to note that all the shoes in the closet, Philip's and Frannie's, sneakers and heels, are jumbled together. Suddenly she stops chattering and says, "I feel like I'm invading you. Are you sure you don't mind?" Frannie laughs and nods and tells her not to worry. "Do you promise to tell me to go home the first moment I get tiresome?" Florence asks.

"I promise!" Her mock exasperation is reassuring.

Florence says that her best friend in college was the most mysterious and beautiful woman she ever met, and the only man who ever treated her friend badly was the one she married. Marriage is something Florence doesn't understand at all. Florence mentions that she has saved over six thousand dollars since nursing school and wants to buy a little house and plant raspberry canes, but the prices of houses rise faster than her savings account. Frannie says, "You know, it really was fascinating to look at houses with Philip. We went out

every day with the realtor, so we really lost the sense of
having our own life, and began to feel like the right house
was the key to everything. On the Sunday morning after we
saw this one, which we both liked, and which was empty,
the agent took us to one a ways out of town. The owners
were there, and they had a new baby, about ten days old.
The place was spotless. There were lots of windows and
awnings, and arched doorways, and the place had a sort of
Provençal aura about it, maybe because the cookbooks were
in French. They took us all over the house, then out into the
yard, where they had planted all sorts of lilacs and the dwarf
apple trees and bulbs. The house was overpriced, and we
would have had to replace the furnace, but Philip fell so in
love that he just had to have it. Even when the realtor told
him this was more of a bargain, Philip couldn't stop talking
about how he felt there—so light and springy. I kept teasing
him and saying he just wanted the chance to live their life
better than they were doing it." She laughs.

"I'm glad you got this house."

"It is beautiful. Philip loves it now."

Florence begins to eye Frannie closely for symptoms of retreat,
but Frannie's interest and growing affection seem to meet
hers at every level. Florence offers to pick up Frannie's cleaning when she is downtown. Frannie brings home butter from
the market, which she knows Florence needs. Florence drops
by next door once a day. Frannie comes by only every other
day or so, but comments spontaneously that she loves it when
people drop by. Where they lived before, everyone was terrifically formal—always calling and making arrangements as
if they expected to be entertained. Every time she sees Frannie, Florence feels intelligent. Her new powers exhilarate her.

Florence crosses the adjoining side yards on a rainy Saturday morning. Frannie is intending to meet Philip at the hardware store and is waiting for the rain to let up. She pours Florence a cup of coffee. "Won't he be annoyed if you're late?" Florence asks, feeling nosy because Frannie just doesn't gossip about her husband in that way; she tells what he does, but never what he is like. Florence thinks this might be the result of so many years together.

"He'll love the chance to moon around the hardware store planning major renovations."

"Say, do you like the yellow slicker effect?" Florence gestures toward the raincoat she has left by the door. "I just bought it at the Army-Navy. It feels like a three-man pup tent, but I love it."

Frannie nods and sips her coffee. There is a letter next to her elbow, and the return address is illegible, although in a woman's hand. In a moment Frannie says, "It's odd, you know. I haven't had a really intimate woman friend since the day Philip and I got married, though I'd had three or four the day before. There's a friend I've had since grammar school, who must know more about me than my mother does, and yet there are these incredibly trivial things about my life and my feelings that I don't dare tell her, not to mention the more important things. It seems like once I let her in, even her, the door will be broken open forever, and Philip will be the loser."

At once Florence has an image of herself standing in the doorway curious and unsure. That's what Frannie means, she thinks. She is so embarrassed that she stays away a whole week, until Frannie comes over the following Saturday afternoon and asks her to go swimming with them, then stay for dinner. She and Philip husk the corn, then she and Frannie take either end of the garlic bread and butter until they meet in the middle. Philip hands her the lettuce to dry, then Frannie turns the spareribs on the grill while Florence bastes them. They drink two six-packs of beer. They eat and drink in the gathering darkness of the side porch for a long time, until at last there are only voices. Sometimes Philip and Frannie speak at once, sometimes Florence and Frannie. Later, Florence falls asleep on the new living room couch, and in the morning, Philip wakes her with hot tea and buttered toast.

September comes, and Florence must work hard. The neonate nursery is jammed and there is a rash of school-related infections among the regular clinic patients. Late in the month she comes down with the virus herself. She spends many evenings on the Howards' wide, deep couch, sipping white wine with her eyes closed and not saying much. Philip often works upstairs in his study while Frannie reads or sews. Florence leafs through magazines and surrenders herself to exhaustion. They have gotten beyond the stage of wild talking and into the stage of companionable silence. Philip and Frannie are not perfect. Philip can be garrulous and tends to repeat some of his jokes. Frannie breaks dates at the last minute because she never writes anything down. Florence doesn't mind, even while feeling annoyed. She is glad that the honeymoon is over and the work of real friendship is about to begin.

In October there are even more newborns, and Florence has to give the hospital Frannie and Philip's number so that she can be called when the other nurses succumb to the virus. October is the best month. It is crisp and dark outside, and the big, neat house folds them in with light and warmth.

In November she volunteers for the second shift through Christmas because it will be more money and she needs a good excuse to get rid of the photographer, whom Frannie and Philip don't think is good enough for her. She calls Frannie at work when she can. After Christmas Frannie tells her that she and Philip are separating.

Florence is very discreet. She tries not to encounter Philip in the neighborhood, and if she sees him before he sees her, she pretends to be occupied. When she absolutely can't avoid him, she speaks cordially, but with a certain distance, as if the sun were in her eyes. She wishes she had a car, so that she might help Frannie with her moving, or that she lived in a big place across town, so that Frannie could stay with her for a while, at least.

Frannie is too happy to confide the details about the separation, and the apartment she finds is very small, very badly furnished. To Florence she says, "But I want a furnished place! It took me days to move my stuff into that empty house. I felt like I was being snapped up like a tasty morsel. This is perfect!" She hangs up her clothes. She speaks continually in the tones Florence remembers from the beginning of their friendship, as if she will abandon herself to merriment at any moment. Florence waits for her to speak about Philip, or rather, about her life with Philip (for she often says now, "Philip must have my comb," or "Philip was in the market this afternoon"), but she never does, even during the intimate moments of sharing dinner preparations or cleaning the previous tenant's leavings out of the closets and cupboards. Florence reminds herself that Frannie has a basic reserve, especially about Philip, and that if anyone is to know, it will certainly be herself. Meanwhile, Frannie's conversation is more earnest than ever. She talks about everything except the recent past.

Some weeks pass. Florence is very curious. She brings

a new boyfriend to Frannie's apartment. When he, in his comradely, once-married, matter-of-fact way, asks Frannie if she thinks she will go back to Philip, Florence sits very still and holds her breath. Frannie shakes her head without a thought. They do not pursue the subject. It is almost as if the question is dull to them, or as if they both know the ins and outs of it so well that they needn't go on. Florence bites her lip at her own curiosity, and her admiration for Bryan, both his experience and his directness, increases. The next day she asks Frannie what she thinks of Bryan, and watches her closely to detect envy in her approval. There is none.

In Sears, they pass a display of ribbed, sleeveless undershirts and baggy shorts. "Philip just loves those," says Frannie.

Such an elderly style seems so incongruous with Philip's natural elegance that Florence guffaws. "No, really!" says Frannie. "The whole family wears that stuff, and Philip's mother irons all their shorts!" After this exchange, Florence feels oddly more hostile toward Philip, which is why, when she sees him on the street a few days later, and he smiles and pauses for a chat, she walks right past him.

Florence spends many evenings with Frannie. She takes the bus and often arrives panting and slapping in a flurry of snow, as if on an adventure. She stays the night on the living room floor. "I wish you'd visit me!" she asserts. "I could sneak you in and out under cover of darkness." Frannie never comes, though, and it is just as well. Nothing about Florence's carefully arranged, thoughtfully acquired apartment is as hospitable as Frannie's temporary rooms.

They make popcorn and crack beers, then turn out the lights and position their chairs before the bay window. Cars and semis rush past on the main thoroughfare nearby, and they make plans to jog, to swim, to learn to cook Middle Eastern food. Florence talks about Bryan. Most of her remarks are open-ended, so that Frannie can simply fall into telling all about it if she wants to. She doesn't, even when Florence says, "If you ever want to talk about what happened, you can trust me completely. You know that, don't you?" Frannie always nods.

Florence can hardly help speculating, especially at home, alone in her own kitchen, staring out at Philip's stained-glass windows. The thumps and sawings that occasionally sound from his house seem to her not the mysteries of the moment, but those of the past autumn, when she was so often inside, but never saw what was going on.

She picks at the burned kernels in the bottom of the popcorn bowl. "You know what one of the mothers said to me today? They'd done Lamaze, I guess, she and her husband, and she said that when the pains got bad, he climbed up onto the labor table and held her head in his arms. She looked me full in the face and asked, 'How can my marriage not be perfect from now on? We were splendid together!' "

"Philip and I lost a baby." Frannie tips the beer can back and catches the last drops with her tongue. Florence runs one of the kernels around and around the buttery bowl. This is the moment. What Florence wishes to know is the story of their mundaneness: what was said over breakfast, and in what tone, what looks were exchanged, what noises Frannie could not help listening to when she was tending her own affairs, who would be the first to break a silence. "I was prediabetic without knowing it. She went full term, but when we got to the hospital they said she had died in labor, then knocked me out." Frannie speaks calmly, expecting Florence's expertise to fill in the details, which, regrettably, it does.

"They should have suspected." She is professionally disapproving.

"The doctor was an ass. It was a long time ago. Almost eight years."

Needless to say, it was tragic, devastating, but how so? Florence sips her beer and glances into Frannie's face. No more on the subject is forthcoming.

Bryan joins them twice, but though he likes Frannie, his pleasure in her company isn't as exquisite as Florence expects it to be. That he might sometimes be on the verge of criticizing Frannie annoys her, because she is beginning to have so much fun with him that it can no longer be called "fun." It encompasses many things other than, and opposite to, amusement.

He tells lots of stories. His past begins to assume the proportions of an epic to Florence. She likes his self-confidence and his ready flow of conversation, his thick, curly hair, and his willingness to be teased. She listens to all his stories with interest, but when he talks about his ex-wife, she can't keep her attention on what he is saying. Images of Frannie, Philip, their pale furniture and their pale floors invade her imagination. "Marriage is such a mystery to me," she says idly.

"Well, it's a mystery to me, too, even though I sometimes think I can remember every minute of my own."

"And you're going to describe them all, one by one?" She smiles.

"Only if you ask."

"And besides, there's so much else to cover." She pokes him in the ribs.

"You don't want to hear it?"

"Every word, every word."

"The past is always with you."

"God forbid." But she doesn't mean it. She will remember, for example, every moment of this talk—the fall
of light through the hackberry bushes fixes his words and his
tones permanently; his words and tones do the same for the
light.

At the hospital, she surprises herself by recalling things
she did not know she had noticed—the color of his socks,
the titles of the books piled on his dashboard, what he almost
ordered for dinner but decided against. When she relates
these details to Frannie, Frannie's smile reminds her that she
is like the one- and two-day mothers who tell her exactly
how the breast was taken, whether the sucking reflex seemed
sufficiently developed, how five minutes on each side didn't
seem like enough. Like the mothers, Florence smiles, self-
deprecating, but can't stop.

"Another thing about him," she tells Frannie on the
phone, "is that he acts as much as he talks. Don't you think
that's very rare? We never sit around, saying what shall we
do. When he picks me up, he always has some plan. And
he thinks about what I might like to do, and he's always
right. I must say that this care is rather thrilling. It's almost
unmasculine!"

"I'm envious," replies Frannie, and Florence, marveling
at her good luck, demurs. "He does have something of a
temper, though." When Florence hangs up the phone, she
realizes that Frannie didn't sound envious. Florence smiles.
She loves Frannie completely.

That evening Bryan says, "Doesn't your friend Frannie
work over at the U?"

"Off-campus programs. How come?"

"Someone mentioned her at lunch today."

"What did they say?" Her voice rises, oddly protective and angry. Bryan glances at her and smiles. "Nothing, dear. Just mentioned her name."

Florence remains disturbed and later decides it is because she wants Frannie, Frannie's delight, conversation, thoughtfulness, all to herself. That her name can come up among strangers implies a life that fans away into the unknown. She wonders about Frannie's activities in the intervals of her absence. She feels none of this jealousy with Bryan.

Florence rolls away from Bryan and grabs the phone at the end of the first ring. Bryan heaves and groans but does not awaken. Florence thinks it will be the hospital, but it is Frannie, who says, "My Lord, it's only ten thirty!"

"I got up at five this morning. How are you?"

"Can you get up at six tomorrow? A friend offered me her strawberry patch. We can pick some, then have a picnic breakfast."

"Lovely. Let's just have fruit and bread and juice."

"I'll pick you up at six fifteen."

"Mmmmm."

The morning could not be fresher. Frannie's new car is pearled with dew and smells, inside, of French bread. The strawberry patch is professionally laid out in neat rows, and among shiny dark leaves, the heartlike berries weigh into pale straw. The earth is springy and smells of damp. Two maples at the corner of the garden cast black, sharp-edged shadows; everything else sparkles with such sunlight that Florence's vision vibrates. Ripe berries plop into their hands at a touch. Frannie, it turns out, has brought champagne. "And not only jam," she is saying, "but a really delicious liqueur my friend has the recipe for. And look over there!

Those two apricot trees bloomed this spring, and that peach. The one next to it is a Chinese chestnut. She lives here alone and hates to see it go to waste. In the fall, she says she has the best apples in the county." Frannie shades her eyes and looks across the field toward the house. "I was hoping she'd come out. Anyway, last year there were seven bushels on one tree alone."

"Frannie, I've known you all these months, and I've never realized what an earth mother you are. I feel like I've missed something."

"Converts are the most ardent, you know. But don't you love the romance of the harvest?" She sucks a berry off the stem.

"The romance of putting up two dozen quarts of to-matoes and a dozen quarts of beans in one evening when the temperature and the humidity are both ninety-five?"

"The romance of opening a jar of strawberry jam in the middle of December!"

"I'd call that the romance of consumption."

"Call it what you like. Mmmmm!" She bites into an-other strawberry and glances toward the still house again.

They sit under one of the maples with their shoes off, tearing hunks of bread. Champagne sizzles in their bowl of berries, and the butter is still cool, dewy. Florence is excited. She thinks she will penetrate the marriage mystery at last, then is ashamed of her unseemly curiosity. Still . . . She says, "Bryan and I saw Philip yesterday." A lie.

"How is Bryan, anyway? Are you in love yet?"

"We've agreed not to say. He's very compelling, though. Especially at six a.m., when I think he's asleep, and he grabs my foot as I'm sneaking out of bed. I thought I was going to jump right out of my skin."

"Do you talk?"

"Nonstop."

There is a pause here, where Frannie might mention her conversational history with Philip, but instead she rolls over and closes her eyes. Florence presses ahead. "I actually spoke to him, Philip I mean. I said hello, he said hello, Bryan said hello." She looks at Frannie. Nothing. "He's so boyish-looking. From a distance he looks about eighteen, and getting younger. That's another thing about Bryan. Being prematurely grizzled makes him look very wise. Are you asleep?"

Frannie shakes her head and slips her hand into the bowl. "Mmmmm," she says.

"Do you ever miss him?" This is so bold that Florence blushes.

Frannie shrugs. "How's Bryan's work going?" Bryan's work is to figure out how many ways the hospital can use the computer it has just purchased.

"Terrifically," says Florence. "Now they're thinking of renting time to the county and making a profit on the purchase."

"But they bought it with county money."

"The left hand doesn't know what the right hand is doing." Florence sighs. "You know, you always turn the conversation over to me, and I always rise to the bait."

"More strawberries?" Frannie holds out the bowl, and Florence gives up. They talk about a movie Frannie wants to go to, then about the seven-pound twins Florence saw the previous week. Florence begins to think of Bryan and to wonder what time it is. The champagne in the bottom of the crystal bowl is flat. Just then Frannie says, "I hate the way Philip and I admired ourselves all the time."

Florence picks up the napkins and the champagne cork and the wrappings from the loaf of bread, and then it is time to depart.

"Well, I don't think life has passed *me* by." Florence, in her bathrobe, strikes a pose on the stairs. Bryan looks up from his book, elaborately distracted. Florence lifts her chin. Lately, they have been debating whether life has passed Bryan by.

"No, bitch," he says, just containing a smile. "Life hasn't passed you by." Florence exhibits an ostentatious bit of calf. "You were standing in the road, and it ran you right over!" Florence laughs and runs up the steps. At the top, she hits the light switch, plunging Bryan into darkness, then she throws herself diagonally across the bed.

When Bryan comes in, she is pretending to be asleep. He walks around the bed. "I'm so comfortable," she groans. "You'll have to sleep on the floor." She stretches out her arms. "There's no room."

"I see a spot," he says. She can hear the smile in his voice, and she feels her body contract with the tension of imminent laughter. Then he launches himself diagonally across her. The weight of his body is delightful: for a moment they are still, and she seems to feel the muffled beat of his heart. Then they are laughing and floundering across one another. They have been laughing all evening, and this laughter, Florence knows, will bloom smoothly into lovemaking. "I love you," he says. He has said it often lately.

"Do you mind if I reciprocate at once?"

"Not at all."

"I love you, too."

"Ah." They snuggle down and pull up the covers.

Just when Florence thinks it is about to begin, when

her skin seems to rise to meet the palm of his hand, he squeezes her closely and says, "Speaking of love."

"Please do."

"Your friend seems to have a new one."

"Which friend?" Florence's eyes are closed, and she is trying to guess where his hands are, where they will alight.

"Frannie," he says.

Florence opens her eyes and sits up. "Oh, really?" she says. "Who?" And then, in a less casual tone, "She didn't tell me."

"A woman in the art school, I think."

"Which part do you think?"

"What?"

"What's questionable, love, art school, or woman?"

"Art school."

"Oh."

"I thought you'd be glad. They look very happy. I saw them having tea this afternoon."

"Oh."

"I'm sorry I told you."

"Don't be."

"Come here. Please. We've had such a good time to-night."

"We really have." She kisses him on the nose and smiles, but in the end they settle into bed without making love. Florence says, "I think if we hadn't had such a good time tonight then I wouldn't be able to imagine their every moment together." But she says it quietly, knowing that Bryan has fallen asleep.

She'd intended to drop in at Frannie's the next morning, a Saturday, on her way to the store, but now that seems like she'd be rushing by for the details. She doesn't know what she would say, all she can think of are challenges and accusations.

She stops on the way home, leaving Bryan's car at the end of the block. No one is around, and she sees that Frannie's belongings are in the street—the plant stand, two boxes of books; clothes in a large pile seem especially vulnerable. Florence looks around for Frannie's winter coat to throw over them, but she can't find it. While she is standing there, Frannie's car pulls up. The other woman is with her, and Frannie's "Hello!" is wildly exuberant. Florence attributes this to the presence of the other woman.

Frannie introduces them. The woman's name, Helen Meardon, is certainly conservative, even old-fashioned, and her thighs are too fat. Otherwise she is very pretty. Florence listens for Helen Meardon to say, "I've heard so much about you," but she does not, in fact, smile again after the introduction, although her inspection of Florence, whose clothes are a mess and whose hair is dirty, is frank and lengthy. Helen Meardon is a person of style. "I didn't know you were moving," Florence says heartily, thinking of a recent evening together.

"Darling! It's very sudden. The house is terrific! Remember where we went for strawberries? Helen's just put in the most beautiful red enameled wood-burning stove. It's practically her place, she moved in so long ago, and the rent hasn't been raised in years, so it should cost next to nothing to live there."

"That's great."

"You'll have to come over as soon as you can."

"I'm so surprised."

Helen Meardon is moving away, toward the apartment

building. She exchanges with Florence a suspicious sidelong glance before passing her and climbing the porch steps.

"Maybe I will come over," asserts Florence.

"Or we could have lunch together downtown."

"Can I help you move? I've got Bryan's car."

"We can handle it, I think," announces Helen from the porch. "We're nearly finished." She goes into the building.

"Helen's terribly shy," says Frannie, looking after her. "You must be good friends with her to be moving in."

"We met almost my first week on the job last fall. Sometimes I feel like I've known her since kindergarten, and sometimes I feel like we've just met."

"Mmm."

"Frannie! What about this?" Helen is holding an object up at the window screen. Frannie turns to squint at it.

"I better go. Bryan will be expecting his lunch," Florence says.

Frannie smiles at her.

"Not that I'll make it for him, I mean. I'm not his slave, of course. I just went to the store."

Frannie continues to smile. "He's a nice man."

"I think we're in love now."

"You told me that last week."

"Yes, right." It is impossible to leave. At length, Florence simply turns away and runs down the street to the car. She imagines Frannie and Helen meeting in the doorway of the empty apartment, the same height, kissing.

Florence is drawn outside by the odors of cut grass and privet. Bryan should be coming soon to take her swimming. It is a glorious day, and Philip is snipping his hedge, his back to her, his progress slow and neat. The grass he has mown is already bagged and sitting on the curb. Before going back inside, Florence watches him for a minute. She hasn't spoken to him since her spring antagonism. Now she fears that she has found out the secret of his marriage, and he would know by looking at her.

He sets down his shears and wipes his face in his shirt. When she turns to go inside, he calls to her, "What do you think, Florence, shall I trim it into birds and perfect spheres?"

"What is that called again?"

"Topiary. How's the baby business?"

"Bouncing. How are you?"

"Sorry not to see you more often. And this is your slow season."

"I haven't been home much, I'll admit."

"Ah, love." He speaks with only ordinary irony.

"I've been around enough to hear a lot of thumps and bangings across the way. Are you haunted over there?"

"Only by the spirit of remodeling. I took out the kitchen bar and put down new linoleum, and let's see, put in some new windows and repainted a little."

"My goodness!"

"Would you like to see it?"

He has also had a new sofa re-covered in a pattern of green leaves and lemons. The place is even more spacious now than before, if that is possible. Philip's furniture, director's chairs and yellow canvas deck chairs, recalls the ocean. His floors recall sandy beaches. Nothing recalls Frannie, and Florence feels suddenly calmer. He has brought his desk downstairs and set it up where he can survey his solitary realm. There is an air of satisfaction about the furnishings and their arrangement, as if they have spread themselves this way and that, unhindered. "I should have come over sooner,"

Florence says, not remembering till then that she wasn't invited to come over. Still, she feels that she has missed the transformation itself, and having missed it, she will never know what it was that has been transformed. "You know how nosy I am," she adds.

But Philip has gone to the kitchen window. "Look over there. See that little building? I bought that at a farm sale for thirty dollars. It's an old chicken house. Sound, though. I'm insulating it, and putting down a tile floor, then I'm going to install a Franklin stove and run lights out there and make it into my study. No phone, no nothing. Grapes growing all over it, a couple of easy chairs, a nice rug."

"You've got all this space to yourself right here!"

He glances at her, amused that she hasn't gotten the point, and shrugs. "The spirit of remodeling is pretty persistent, you know."

"It's so different from the way it was," she says, because Philip's cool realm oddly invites confidences in a way that Frannie's hospitality did not, "and it's not that I don't like it. It's refreshing. But I loved the rusty-red sofa, and all the chairs drawn up around the coffee table. That kitchen bar was so ugly—awful nineteen fifties modernizing—but it really made the place cozy." Philip is looking at her quizzically. "Don't you think it was nice to just sit around in the evening with most of the lights off and drink brandy and talk? I loved it! Especially when it rained or snowed those times, and even my apartment seemed too far away. Didn't you like it?"

"Our friendship was very pleasant."

"I didn't feel like just your friend. I felt like your child or your sister, or something. Should I be embarrassed? Those nights seemed so self-contained."

"Frannie mooning over Helen, me mooning over Frannie." He speaks with a teasing edge. "I don't think we were very kind to you, Florence."

"Weren't you? I thought you were." Florence swallows bitterly.

"We needed someone else to talk to, about unimportant things."

Florence turns away quickly and peers energetically out the window.

"We needed you, Florence; it was nice to have you fall in love with us, and admire us. It was a relief to talk about something else besides the central issue. Do you understand what I mean?"

"No one was happy but me?" She looks at him again and he shakes his head.

The smile that lingers on his boyish face is betrayed by that small gesture, disappears. Florence lets his serious gaze hold her until he releases her with another smile.

Bryan pulls up next door and gets out of the car. Florence does not move. "Is that the secret of marriage?" she asks.

"One of them."

Bryan takes off his sunglasses and throws them on the seat, then steps around the car.

"What's another one?"

"Maybe that all the secrets are never disclosed."

"And another?"

"That it's worth finding out for yourself."

Bryan raises his finger to her doorbell. She shouts, "Here I am! Bryan, I'm over here!"

Lily

Careering toward Lily Stith in a green Ford Torino were Kevin and Nancy Humboldt. Once more they gave up trying to talk reasonably; once more they sighed simultaneous but unsympathetic sighs; once more each resolved to stare only at the unrolling highway.

At the same moment, Lily was squeezing her mop into her bucket. Then she straightened up and looked out the window, eager for their arrival. She hadn't seen them in two years, not since having won a prestigious prize for her poems.

She was remarkably well made, with golden skin, lit by the late-afternoon sun, delicately defined muscles swelling over slender bones, a cloud of dark hair, a hollow at the base of her neck for some jewel. She was so beautiful that you could not help attributing to her all of your favorite virtues. To Lily her beauty seemed a senseless thing, since it gained her nothing in the way of passion, release, kinship, or intimacy. Now she was looking forward, with resolve, to making the Humboldts confess really and truly what was wrong with her—why, in fact, no one was in love with her.

A few minutes later they pulled up to the curb. Nancy

climbed the apartment steps bearing presents—a jar of dill pickles she had made herself, pictures of common friends, a cap knitted of rainbow colors for the winter. Lily put it on in spite of the heat. The rich colors lit up Lily's tanned face and flashing teeth. Almost involuntarily Nancy exclaimed, "You look better than ever!" Lily laughed and said, "But look at you! Your hair is below your hips now!" Nancy pirouetted and went inside before Kevin came up. He, too, looked remarkable, Lily thought, with his forty-eight-inch chest on his five-foot-nine-inch frame. Kevin kissed her cheek, but she could see he was trying to imagine where Nancy had gone; his eyes slid instantly past Lily and only manners brought them back. He patted her twice on the shoulder when she cried, "I've been looking for you since noon!" He said, "I always forget how far it is across Ohio," and stepped into the house.

That it had been two years—two years!—grew to fill the room like a thousand balloons, pinning them in the first seats they chose and forbidding conversation. Lily offered some food, some drink. They groaned, thinking of all they had eaten on the road (not convivially but bitterly, snatching, biting, swallowing too soon). Lily, assuming they knew what they wanted, did not ask again. Immediately Kevin's hands began to fidget for a glass to jiggle and balance and peer into, to turn slowly on his knee. Two years! Two days! Had they really agreed to a two-day visit?

Although the apartment was neat and airy, the carpet vacuumed and the furniture polished, Lily apologized for a bowl and a plate unwashed beside the sink. Actually, she often wondered whether cleanliness drove love away. Fastidious, she suspected that life itself was to be found in dirt and disorder, in unknown dark substances that she was hesitant to touch. Lily overestimated her neatness in this case. The windowsills, for example, had not been vacuumed, and the leaves of the plants were covered with dust. She began to apologize for the lack of air conditioning, the noise of cars and trucks through the open windows, the weather, the lack of air conditioning again; then she breathed a profound sigh and let her hands drop limply between her knees.

Nancy Humboldt was moved by this gesture to remember how Lily always had a touch of the tragic about her. It was unrelated to anything that had ever happened, but it was distinct, always present. Nancy sat forward and smiled affectionately at her friend. Conversation began to pick up.

After a while they ate. Lily noticed that when Kevin carried his chest toward Nancy, Nancy made herself concave as she sidestepped him. Perhaps he did not exactly try to touch her; the kitchenette was very small. Jokes were much in demand, greeted with pouncing hilarity; a certain warmth, reminiscent of their early friendship, flickered and established itself. Conversation ranged over a number of topics. Nancy kept using the phrase "swept away." "That movie just swept me away!" "I live to be swept away!" "I used to be much more cautious than I am now; now I just want to be swept away!" Kevin as often used the word "careful." "I think you have to be really careful about your decisions." "I'm much more careful now." "I think I made mistakes because I wasn't careful." Lily listened most of the time. When the discussion became awkwardly heated, they leaped as one flesh on Lily and demanded to know about her prizewinning volume, her success, her work. Nancy wanted to hear some new pieces.

Lily was used to reading aloud. Finishing the fourth poem, she wondered, as she often did, why men did not come up to her after readings and offer love, or at least ask her out. She had won a famous prize. Within the intimacy of art she phrased things that she would not ordinarily admit to, discussed her soul, which seemed a perfectly natural and even attractive soul. People liked her work; they had bought more copies of her prizewinning volume than of any other in the thirteen-year series. But no one, in a fan letter, sent a picture or a telephone number. Didn't art or accomplishment make a difference? Was it all invisible? Lily said, "I think Kevin was bored."

"Not at all, really."

"I wasn't in the slightest," Nancy said. "They're very good. They don't have any leaves on them." She laughed and looked around, pleased with her own phrase.

Now was the time to broach her subject, thought Lily. The Humboldts had known her since college. Perhaps they had seen some little thing, spoken of it between themselves, predicted spinsterhood. Lily straightened the yellow pages and set them on the side table. "You know," she said with a laugh and a cough, "I haven't gone out in a month and a half. I mean, I realize it's summer and all, but anyway. And the last guy was just a friend, I—" She looked up and went on. "All those years with Ken, nobody even made a pass at me in a bus station. I didn't think it was important then, but now I've gotten rather anxious."

"Do you ever hear from Ken?" Nancy asked.

"I changed my number and didn't give him the new one. I think he got the message."

"I'll never understand why you spent—"

"Nine years involved with a married man, blah blah blah. I know."

"Among other things."

"When we were breaking up, I made up a lot of reasons,

but now I remember what it was like before we met. It was
just like it is now."

"Everyone has dateless spells, honey," said Nancy, who'd
had her first dateless spell after her marriage to Kevin. She
had always attributed to Lily virginal devotion to her work.
Nancy thought a famous prize certainly equaled a husband
and three children. Love was like any activity, you had to
put in the hours, but as usual Kevin was right there, so she
didn't say this and shifted with annoyance in her chair. "Really,"
she snapped, "don't worry about it."

Kevin's jaws widened in an enormous yawn. Lily jumped
up to find clean towels, saying, "Does it seem odd to you?"
Kevin went into the bathroom and Nancy went into the
bedroom with her suitcase. Lily followed her. "I have no way
of knowing," she went on, but then she stopped. Nancy
wasn't really listening.

In the morning Nancy braided and wound up her hair while
Lily made breakfast. Kevin was still asleep. Nancy had always
had long, lovely hair, but Lily couldn't remember her taking
such pride in it as she was now, twisting and arranging it
with broad, almost conceited motions. She fondled it, put
it here and there. "It looks great in a long upswept braid,"
she said. "And there's a woman I go to who French-braids
it. Then all the colors come out."

"You've kept it in wonderful shape," Lily said.

"My hair is my glory," Nancy replied, and sat down to
her eggs. She was not kidding.

When Kevin staggered from bedroom to bathroom an
hour later, Nancy had gone out to survey the local shops.
Kevin looked for her in every room of the apartment and
then said, "Nancy's not here?"

"She thought she'd have a look around."

Kevin dropped into his seat at the table and put his head in his arms. A second later he exclaimed, "Oh, God!" Lily liked Kevin better this visit than she had before. His chest, which had always seemed to drag him aggressively into situations, had lost some of its influence. He was not as loud or blindingly self-confident as he had been playing football, sitting in the first row in class, then, later, barreling through business school, swimming two miles every day. Once, in a car, she had heard him mutter to her date, "I wouldn't mind a good fight right now." Thus it was with sympathy rather than astonishment that Lily realized he was weeping. He wiped his eyes on his T-shirt. "She's going to leave me! When we get back to Vancouver, she's going to leave me for another guy!"

"Is that what she said?"

"I know."

"Did she say so?"

"I know."

"Look, sit up a second and have this piece of toast."

"He's just a dumb cowboy. I know she's sleeping with him."

She put food in front of him and he began to eat it. After a few bites, though, he pushed it away and put his head down. He moaned into the cave of his arms. Lily said, "What?"

"She won't sleep with me. She hasn't since Thanksgiving. She never says where she's going or when she'll be back. She can't stand me checking up on her."

"Do you check up on her?"

"I call her at work sometimes. I just want to talk to her. She never wants to talk to me. I miss her!"

"What do Roger and Fred say?" Roger and Fred were friends from college who also lived in Vancouver, though no longer with Kevin and Nancy, as they had.

"They don't understand."

Lily nodded. Unlike Lily, Roger and Fred had wavered in their fondness for Nancy. Many times Nancy had been selfish about certain things, which were perhaps purely feminine things. She thought people should come to the table when dinner was hot in spite of just-opened beers and half-smoked cigarettes, or unfinished repair projects in the driveway. She had screamed, really screamed, about booted feet on her polished table. Roger and Fred especially found her too punctilious about manners, found her slightly shrill, and did not appreciate her sly wit or her generosity with food and lodging and presents (this liberality they attributed to Kevin, who was, actually, a famous tightwad). And they overlooked her capacity for work—her willing, organized, unsnobbish bringing home of the bacon while all the men were looking for careers and worrying about compromising themselves. Lily and Kevin at least agreed that Nancy was a valuable article.

"Okay," Lily said, "who's the dumb cowboy?"

"His name is Hobbs Nolan. She met him at a cross-country ski clinic last year. But he's not really outdoorsy or athletic; he just wears these pointy-toed cowboy boots and flannel cowboy shirts. Out there guys like him are a dime a dozen . . ."

"You know him?"

"I've seen him. He knows people we know. They think he's a real jerk."

"You blame him for all of this, then?"

Kevin glanced at her and said, "No." After a moment

he exclaimed "Oh, God!" again, and dropped his head on his arms. His hair grazed the butter dish, and Lily was suddenly repelled by these confidences. She turned and looked out the window, but Nancy was nowhere in sight. The freshness of the morning was gone, and the early blue sky had whitened. She looked at her watch. It was about ten thirty. Any other morning she would already be sitting down to her work with an apple and a cup of tea, or she would be strolling into town with her list of errands. She glanced toward the bedroom. The blanket was half off the bed and a corner of the contour sheet had popped off the mattress. Nancy's and Kevin's clothes were piled on the floor. They had left other items in the living room or the kitchen: Nancy's brush, a scarf, Kevin's running shoes and socks, two or three pieces of paper from Nancy's purse, the map on which they had traced their route. But hadn't she expected and desired such intimacy? He sat up. She smiled and said, "You know, you're the first people to spend the night here in ages. I'd forgotten—"

"I don't think you should worry about that. Like Nancy said, we all go through dry spells. Look at me, my—"

"Oh, that! I wasn't referring to that."

"My whole life was a dry spell before Nancy came along."

Lily sat back and looked at Kevin. He was sighing. "Hey," she said, "you're going to have a lot better luck if you lighten up a little."

"I know that, but I can't." He sounded petulant.

Lily said, "Well—"

"Well, now I'd better go running before it gets too hot." Kevin reached for his shoes and socks. But Nancy walked in and he sat up without putting them on. Nancy displayed her packages. "There was a great sale on halter tops, and look at this darling T-shirt!" She pulled out an example of the T-shirt Lily had seen on everyone all summer. It said "If you live a good life, go to church, and say your prayers, when you die you will go to OHIO." Lily smiled. Nancy tossed the T-shirt over to Kevin, saying, "Extra extra large. I'm sure it will fit."

He held it up and looked at it and then said, glumly, "Thanks."

"Are you going for your run now?"

"Yeah."

But he didn't make a move. Everyone sat very still for a long time, maybe five minutes, and then Lily began clearing plates off the table and Nancy began to take down her hair. Kevin seemed to root himself in the chair. His face was impassive. Nancy glared at him, but finally sighed and said, "I got a long letter from Betty Stern not so long ago. She stopped working on her Chinese dissertation and went to business school last year."

"I heard that Harry got a job, but that it was in Newfoundland or someplace like that," Lily said.

"Who'd you hear that from?" Refusing even to look in Kevin's direction, Nancy combed her hair.

"Remember Meredith Lawlor? Did you know she was here? She's teaching in the pharmacy school here in Columbus. She raises all these poisonous tropical plants in a big greenhouse she and her husband built out in the country."

"Who's her husband?"

"She met him in graduate school, I think. He's from Arizona."

"I'd like to raise plants for a living. I don't know necessarily about poisonous ones." Nancy glanced at Kevin. Lily noticed that she had simply dropped her packages by her chair, that tissue paper and sales slips and the halter tops themselves were in danger of being stepped on. In college they had teased Nancy relentlessly about her disorderly ways, but Lily hadn't found them especially annoying then. Kevin said, "Why don't you pick that stuff up before you step on it?"

"I'm not going to step on it!"

"Well, pick it up anyway. I doubt that Lily wants your mess all over her place."

"Who are you to speak for Lily?"

"I'm speaking for society in general, in this case."

"Why don't you go running, for God's sake?"

"I'd rather not have a heart attack in the heat, thank you."

"Well, it's not actually that hot. It's not as hot as it was yesterday, and you ran seven miles."

"It's hot in here."

"Well, there's a nice breeze outside, and this town is very shady. When you get back we can have lunch after you shower. We can have that smoked turkey we got at the store last night. I still have some of the bread I made the day we left."

Kevin looked at her suspiciously, but all he said finally was, "Well, pick up that stuff, okay?"

Nancy smiled. "Okay."

Still Kevin was reluctant to go, tying his shoes with painful slowness, drinking a glass of water after letting the tap run and run, retying one of his shoes, tucking and un-tucking his shirt. He closed the door laboriously behind him, and Nancy watched out the window for him to appear on the street. When he did, she inhaled with sharp, exasperated relief. "Christ!" she exclaimed.

"He doesn't seem very happy."

"But you know he's always been into that self-dramatization. I'm not impressed. I used to be, but I'm not anymore."

Lily wondered how she was going to make it to lunch, and then through the afternoon to dinner and bedtime. Nancy turned toward her. "I shouldn't have let all these men talk to you before I did."

"What men?"

"Kevin, Roger, Fred."

"I haven't talked to Roger or Fred since late last winter, at least."

"They think I ought to be shot. But they really infuriate me. Do you know what sharing a house with Roger was like? He has the most rigid routine I have ever seen, and he drives everywhere, even to the Quick Shop at the end of the block. I mean, he would get in his car and drive out the driveway and then four houses down to pick up the morning paper. And every time he did the dishes, he broke something we got from our wedding, and then he would refuse to pay for it because we had gotten it for free anyway.

"Fred and I get along, but in a way I think he's more disapproving than Roger is. Sometimes he acts as if I've shocked him so much that he can't bear to look at me."

"So how have you shocked him?"

"Didn't Kevin tell you about Hobbs Nolan?"

"He mentioned him."

"But Hobbs isn't the real issue, as far as I'm concerned. Men always think that other men are the real issue. You know, Roger actually sat me down one night and started to tell me off?"

"What's the real issue?"

"Well, one thing I can't bear is having to always report in whenever I go somewhere. I mean, I get in the car to go for groceries, and if I decide while I'm out to go to the mall, Kevin expects me to call and tell him. Or if I have to work even a half hour late, or if the girl I work with and I decide to go out for a beer after work. I hate it. I hate picking up the goddamned telephone and dialing all the numbers. I hate listening to it ring, and most of all I hate that automatic self-justification you just slide into. I mean, I don't know how to sound honest anymore, even when I'm being honest."

"Are you—"

"No, most of all I hate the image I have of Kevin the whole time I'm talking to him, sitting home all weekend with nothing to do, whining into the phone."

"I think Kevin is mostly upset because you don't sleep with him."

"Well—"

"I really don't see how you can cut him off like that."

"Neither does he."

"Why do you?"

"Don't you think he's strange-looking? And everything he does in bed simply repels me. It didn't used to but now it does. I can't help it. He doesn't know how big or strong he is and he's always hurting me. When I see him move toward me, I wince. I know he's going to step on me or poke me or bump into me."

"Well, you could go to a therapist. You ought to at least reassure Kevin that you're not sleeping with this other guy."

"We did go to a therapist, and he got so nervous he was even more clumsy, and I *am* sleeping with Hobbs."

"Nancy!"

"Why are you surprised? How can this be a reason for surprise? I'm a sexual person. Kevin always said that he thought I was promiscuous until I started with him, and then he just thought that I was healthy and instinctive."

"Well, Nancy—"

"I have a feeling you aren't very approving either."

"I don't know, I—"

"But that's all I want. I realized on the way here that all the time I've known you I've wanted you to approve of me. Not just to like me, or even respect me, but to approve of me. I still like being married to Kevin, but all of us know by now that the best person for being married to isn't always the best person for sleeping with, and there's no reason why he should be." She glanced out the window. "Anyway, here he comes." A moment later the door slammed open. Lily thought Kevin was angry, until she realized that he had simply misjudged the weight of the door. Sweat was pouring off him, actually dripping on the carpet. Nancy said, "Jesus! Go take a shower." Lily wanted to tell him not to drip over the coffee table, with its bowl of fruit, but said nothing. He looked at them with studied ingenuousness and said, "Four miles in twenty-five minutes. Not bad, huh? And it's ninety-three. I just ran past the bank clock."

"Great." Nancy turned back to Lily and said, "Maybe I should try to call Meredith Lawlor while I'm here. We were pretty good friends junior year. I've often thought about her, actually." Kevin tromped into the bathroom.

Drying lettuce for the sandwiches, Lily watched Nancy slice the turkey. It was remarkable, after all, how the other woman's most trivial mannerisms continued to be perfectly familiar to her after two years, after not thinking about Nancy or their times together for days and even weeks at a stretch. It was as if the repeated movement of an arm through the air or the repeated cocking of a head could engrave itself willy-nilly on her brain, and her brain, recognizing what was already contained in it, would always respond with warmth. In fact, although she did feel this burr of disapproval toward Nancy and sympathy for Kevin, Kevin's presence was oppressive and Nancy's congenial. Nancy got out the bread she had made, a heavy, crumbly, whole-grain production, and they stacked vegetables and meat on the slices and slathered them with mustard and catsup. The shower in the bathroom went off and Nancy sighed. Lily wondered if she heard herself.

Lily remembered that the kitchen workers in the college cafeteria had always teased Kevin about his appetite. Certainly he still ate with noise and single-minded gusto. His lettuce crunched, his bread fell apart, pieces of tomato dropped on his plate and he wiped them up with more bread. He drank milk. Lily tried to imagine him at work. Fifteen months before, he had graduated from business school near the top of his class and had taken a risky job with a small company. The owner was impressed with his confidence and imagination. In a year he'd gotten four raises, all of them substantial. Lily imagined him in a group of men, serious, athletic, well dressed, subtly dominating. Was it merely talking about him that made him seem to eat so foolishly, so dependently, with such naked anxiety? To *be* so foolish, so dependent? When he was finished, Nancy asked him whether he was still hungry and said to Lily, "Isn't this good bread? I made up the recipe myself."

"It's delicious."

"I think so. I've thought of baking bread for the health-food store near us. In fact, they asked me to, but I'm not sure it would be very profitable."

"It's nice that they asked you."

"A couple of guys there really like it."

Kevin scowled. Lily wondered if one of these guys was Hobbs Nolan. Nancy went on, "I make another kind, too, an herb bread with dill and chives and tarragon."

"That sounds good."

"It is."

Lily was rather taken aback at Nancy's immodesty. This exchange, more than previous ones, seemed to draw her into the Humboldts' marriage and to implicate her in its fate. She felt a moment's relief that they would be gone soon. She finished her sandwich and stood up to get an apple. It was before one o'clock. More stuff—the towel Kevin had used on his hair, Nancy's sandals, Nancy's other hairbrush—was distributed around the living room. Lily had spent an especially solitary summer, with no summer school to teach and many of her friends away, particularly since the first of August. Some days the only people she spoke to were checkers at the grocery store or librarians. Her fixation on the Humboldts' possessions was a symptom that her solitary life certainly was unhealthy, that she was, after all, turning back into a virgin, as she feared. It was true that her apartment never looked "lived in" and that she preferred it that way. Suddenly she was envious of them; in spite of their suspicions and resentments, their life together had a kind of attractive complexity. Their minds were full of each other. Just then Kevin said, with annoyance, "Damn!" and Nancy shrugged, perfectly taking his meaning.

"There's a great swimming pool here," Lily said. "I've

spent practically the whole summer there. You must have brought your suits?"

Kevin had been diving off the high board steadily for at least forty-five minutes. At first, when Nancy and Lily had been talking about Kenneth Diamond, and Lily's efforts to end that long relationship, Nancy had only glanced at Kevin from time to time. Lily remarked that she had slept with Ken fewer than twenty times in nine years. Nancy stared at her—not in disbelief but in astonishment. Then, for four dives, Nancy did not take her eyes off Kevin. He did a backward double somersault, tucked; a forward one-and-a-half layout; a forward one-and-a-half in pike position; and a double somersault with a half-gainer, which was astonishingly graceful. "I knew he dove in high school," she said, "but I've never seen this." A plump adolescent girl did a swan dive and Kevin stepped onto the board again. Other people looked up, including two of the lifeguards. Perhaps he was unaware that people were looking at him. He was straightforward and undramatic about stepping into his dive. The board seemed to bend in two under his muscular weight and then to fling him toward the blue sky. He attempted a forward two-and-a-half, tuck position, but failed to untuck completely before entering the water. In a moment he was hoisting himself out and heading for the board to try again. Nancy said, "It's amazing how sexy he looks from a distance. All the pieces seem to fit together better. And he really is a good diver. I can't believe he hasn't practiced in all these years."

"Maybe he has."

"Maybe. I mean he looks perfect, and no older than twenty-one. That's how old he was when we first met—

twenty-one. I was dating Sandy Ritter. And you were dating Murray Freed."

"I could have done worse than stick with Murray Freed. But he was so evasive that when Ken approached me in a grown-up, forthright way, I just gave up on Murray. He's got a little graphics company in Santa Barbara, and I hear he spends two or three months of the year living on the beach in Big Sur."

"Well, don't worry about it. I've always thought leisure and beauty were rather overrated, myself." She grinned. "But look at him! He did it! That one was nearly perfect, toes pointed and everything."

"I guess I'm sort of surprised that you think he's funny-looking. Everybody always thought he was good-looking in college."

"Did they? It's hard to remember what he looks like, even when I'm looking at him. I mean, I know what he looks like, but I don't know what I think about it. This diving sort of turns me on, if you can believe that."

"Really?" But Lily realized that she was vulnerable, too, and when Kevin came over, dripping and fit, toweling his hair and shoulders with Lily's own lavender towel, his smile seemed very white, his skin very rosy, and his presence rather welcome.

Actually, it was apparent that they all felt better. Lily had swum nearly half a mile, and Nancy had cooled off without getting her hair wet. Kevin was pleased with the dives he had accomplished and with Nancy's obvious admiration. All three of them had an appetite, and it was just the right time to begin planning a meal. "This is a nice park," Kevin said. "The trees are huge."

"We should get steak," Nancy said.

· · ·

In the bedroom, putting on her clothes, Lily smiled to hear Nancy's laugh followed by a laugh from Kevin. Really, he was a good-humored sort of person. Although she could not have said how the visit had failed that morning, or why it was succeeding right then, she sensed their time filling up with possibilities of things they could do together. She heard Nancy say, "I think the coals must be ready by now," and the slam of the door. She pulled a cotton sweater over her head and went into the kitchen thinking fondly of the Humboldts driving away the next morning with smiles on their faces and reconciliation in their hearts. She hadn't done anything, really, but something had done the trick. Kevin was sitting at the table wrapping onions and potatoes in foil. Lily opened the refrigerator and took out a large stalk of broccoli, which she began to slice for steaming. Kevin had put on a light-blue tailored shirt and creased corduroy slacks. His wet hair was combed back and he had shaved. He said, "Why did you stick with Diamond all those years? I mean"—he looked at her cautiously—"wasn't it obvious that you weren't going to get anything out of it?"

"I got a lot out of it. Ken's problem is that nobody thinks he's anything special but me. I do think he's quite special, though, and I think I got a good education, lots of attention, lots of affection, and lots of time to work. It wasn't what I expected but it wasn't so bad. Though I wish there had been some way to practice having another type of relationship at the same time, or even just having dates."

"What did he think about your winning the prize?"

"I don't know. I broke up with him right after I applied for it, and I didn't read the letter he sent after I got it."

"Last night, you know when you were asking—" Lily glanced up, alert. Kevin coughed. "Well, I thought about something. All the guys were so afraid of you in college. They all talked about you, you know, and watched you from a distance." He faded, then went on, uncertainly. "Your, ah, eyes were so big, you know. It is disconcerting when you—"

But the door opened and Nancy swept in. "The coals are perfect! Are these the steaks in here? I'm famished! Guess what? I got three big ears of corn from your neighbor, who was out in his garden. He's cute. What's his name? He was funny, and awfully nice to me."

"I've never even spoken to the guy," Lily said.

"What do you do? Cross the street when you see an attractive man?"

"It's not that. It's that some curse renders me invisible. But Kevin was about to say something."

He shrugged.

"Put on you by Professor Kenneth Diamond, no doubt," Nancy said. She handed a potato back to Kevin. "Do that one better. The skin shows. Seriously, Lily"—Kevin took the potato back with a careful, restrained gesture—"you can't keep this up. It's impossible. You're the most beautiful woman anyone we know knows. You have to at least act like you're interested. I'm sure you act like you wouldn't go on a date for a million dollars. You don't prostitute yourself simply by being friendly." Kevin rewrapped the potato and handed it back to Nancy. Then he smiled at Lily and she had a brief feeling that something dramatic had been averted, although she couldn't say what it was. Nancy ripped the paper off the rib eyes and dropped it on the table. The Humboldts went outside to put on the meat, and when they came back in, Lily couldn't see how to lead Kevin back to his earlier remark.

The wine was nearly finished. Kevin had chosen it, a California red that he'd tried in Vancouver. He kept saying, "I was lucky to find this so far east. That isn't a bad liquor store, really." Lily hadn't especially liked it at first because of its harsh flavor and thick consistency, but after three glasses she was sorry to see the second bottle close to empty. She set it carefully upright in the grass. There was a mystery to its flavor that made her keep wanting to try it again. Nancy was talking about the play she had been in, as the second lead, with a small theater group in Vancouver. Kevin said, smiling, "She got a lot of applause, too. The third night, she got more than anyone in the cast. She was pretty funny."

"I was very funny."

"Yes, you were very funny."

Nancy lay back on the chaise longue. "The director said that he thought I should take acting classes at the university. They have a very good program. I had never acted before, and they gave me the second lead. You know, there are tons of professional actors in Vancouver."

"It wasn't exactly a professional show. Only the two leads were getting paid, and the guy wasn't even an Equity actor," Kevin said.

"I know that."

Lily took a deep breath. Neither Kevin nor Nancy had changed position in the past five minutes. Both were still leaning back, gazing into the tops of the trees or at the stars, but their voices were beginning to rise. She said, "It must be lovely to live in Vancouver." She thought of it vividly, as if for the first time: thick vegetation, brilliant flowers,

dazzling peaks, lots to eat and do, the kind of paradise teaching would probably never take her to.

"It's expensive," Nancy said. "And I've found the people
very self-satisfied."

"I don't think that's true," Kevin said.

"I know you don't. Kevin likes it there just fine. But
the university is good, and they send acting students off to
places like Yale and England and New York City all the
time."

"By the time you could get into acting school, you
would be thirty-one at the very least." Kevin had sat up now,
but casually. He poured the last of the mysterious-tasting
wine into his glass.

"How do you figure that?"

"Well, frankly, I don't see how you can quit working
for another two years, until I get established." He looked at
the wine in the glass and gulped it down. "And maybe thirty-
one is a little old to start training for a profession where
people begin looking for work before they're out of their
teens. And what about having kids? You can't very well have
any kids while you're going to school full time. That play
had you going eighteen hours a day some days. Which is not
to say that it wasn't worth it, but I don't know that you
would even want to do it six or eight times a year."

Nancy was breathing hard. Lily leaned forward, alarmed
that she hadn't averted this argument, and put her hand on
Nancy's arm. Nancy shook it off. "Kids! Who's talking about
kids? I'm talking about taking some courses in what I like
to do and what some people think I'm good at doing. The
whole time I was in that play you just acted like it was a
game that I was playing. I have news for you—"

"It was a community-theater production! You weren't

putting on Shakespeare or Chekhov, either. And it's not as if Bill Henry had directed in Toronto, much less in New York."

"He's done lights in New York! He did lights on *The Fantasticks!* And on *A Chorus Line!*"

"Big deal."

Nancy leaped to her feet. "I'll tell you something, mister. You owe it to me to put me through whatever school I want to go to, no matter what happens to our relationship or our marriage. I slaved in the purchasing department of that university for three years so that you could go to business school full time. I lived with those crummy friends of yours for four years so we could save on mortgage—"

Lily said, "Nancy—"

Kevin said, "What do you mean, 'no matter what happens to our relationship'? What do you mean by that?"

"You know perfectly well what I mean! Lily knows what I mean, too!"

Lily pressed herself deep into her chair, hoping that neither of them would address her, but Kevin turned to face her. In the darkness his deep-set eyes were nearly invisible, so that when he said, "What did she tell you?" Lily could not decide what would be the best reply to make. He stepped between her and Nancy and demanded, "What did she say?"

"I think you should ask her that."

"She won't tell me anything. You tell me." He took a step toward her. "You tell me whether she still loves me. I want to know that. That's all I want to know." The tone of his voice in the dark was earnest and nearly calm.

"That's between you and Nancy. Ask her. It's not my business."

"But you know. And I've asked her. She's said yes so

many times to that question that it doesn't mean anything anymore. You tell me. Does she still love me?"

"She hasn't told me anything."

"But you have your own opinion, don't you?"

"I can't see that that's significant in any way."

"Tell me what it is. Does she still love me?"

He seemed, with his chest, to be bearing down on her as she sat. She had lost all sense of where Nancy was, even whether she was still outside. Wherever she was, she was not coming to Lily's aid. Perhaps she too was waiting for Lily's opinion. Lily said, "No."

"No, what? Is that your opinion?"

Surely Nancy would have stepped in by now. "No, it doesn't seem to me that she loves you anymore." Lily broke into a sweat the moment she stopped speaking, a sweat of instant regret. Kevin stepped back and Lily saw that Nancy was behind him, still and silent on the chaise longue. "Oh, Lord," said Lily, standing up and taking her glass into the house.

The Humboldts stayed outside for a long time. Lily washed the dishes and got ready for bed; she was sitting on the cot in the guest room winding her clock when Nancy knocked on the door and came in. "We had a long talk," she said, "and things are all right."

"Did you—"

"I don't want to talk about it anymore. This may be the best thing. At least I feel that I've gotten some things clear. And I think we're going to leave very early in the morning, so I wish you wouldn't get up."

"But I—" Lily looked at Nancy for a moment, and then said, "Okay, I won't. Thanks for stopping."

"You can't mean that, but I'll write." She closed the door and Lily put her feet under the sheet. There were no sounds, and after a while she fell asleep. She awoke to a rhythmic knocking. She thought at first of the door, but remembered that Nancy had closed it firmly. Then she realized that the blows were against the wall beside her head. She tried to visualize the other room. It would be the bed, and they would be making love. She picked up her clock and turned it to catch light from the street. It was just after midnight. She had been asleep, although deeply, for only an hour. The knocking stopped and started again, and it was irregular enough to render sleep unlikely for the time being. She smoothed her sheet and blanket and slid farther into the bed. Even after her eyes had adjusted, the room was dark; the streetlight was ten yards down, and there was no moon. Nancy and Kevin's rhythmic banging was actually rather comforting, she thought. She lay quietly for a moment, and then sat up and turned on the light. She felt for her book under the bed. The banging stopped and did not start again, and Lily reached for the light switch, but as her hand touched it, Nancy cried out. She took her hand back and opened her book, and Nancy cried out again. Lily thought of the upstairs neighbor, whom she hadn't heard all evening, and hoped he wasn't in yet. The bed in the next room gave one hard bang against the wall, and Nancy cried out again. Lily grew annoyed at her lack of consideration. She put her feet on the floor. Once she had done that, she was afraid to do anything else. It was suddenly obvious to her that the cries had been cries of fear rather than of passion, and Lily was afraid to go out, afraid of what she might see in the next room. She thought of Kevin's big chest and of Nancy's carelessness about Kevin's feelings. She opened the door. Lights were on everywhere, shocking her, and the noise of some kind of tussle came from their bedroom. Lily crept around the door and peeked in. Kevin had his back to her and was poised with one knee on the bed. All the bedcovers were torn off the bed, and Nancy, who had just broken free, was backed against the window. She looked at Lily for a long second and then turned her head so that Lily could see that her hair had been jaggedly cut off. One side was almost to her shoulder, but the other side stopped at her ear lobe. The skein of hair lay on the mattress. Lily recognized it now. Seeing Nancy's gaze travel past him, Kevin set down a pair of scissors, Lily's very own shears, that had been sitting on the shelf above the sewing machine. Lily said, "My God! What have you been doing?"

Looking for the first time at the hair on the bed, Nancy began to cry. Kevin bent down and retrieved his gym shorts from under the bed and stepped into them. He said to Lily rather than Nancy, "I'm going outside. I guess my shoes are in the living room."

Nancy sat on the bed beside the hair, looking at it. It was reddish and glossy, with the life of a healthy wild animal, an otter or a mink. Lily wished Nancy would say that she had been thinking of having it cut anyway. She thought of saying herself that Nancy could always grow it back, but that, too, was unlikely. Hair like that probably wouldn't grow again on a thirty-year-old head. Lily picked up the shears and put them back on the shelf above her sewing table and said, "You were making love?"

The door slammed. Nancy said, "Yes, actually. I wanted to. We decided to split up." She looked at Lily. "And then when I got in bed I felt happy and free, and I just thought it would be nice."

"And Kevin?"

"He seemed fine! Relieved, even. We were lying there and he was holding me."

"I can't believe you—"

At once Nancy glared at her. "You can't? Why are you so judgmental? This whole day has been one long trial, with you the judge and me the defendant! What do you know, anyway? You've never even lived with anyone! You had this sterile thing with Kenneth Diamond that was more about reading poems than screwing and then you tell my husband that I'm not in love with him anymore! Of course he was enraged. You did it! You hate tension, you hate conflict, so you cut it off, ended it. We could have gone on for years like this, and it wouldn't have been that bad!"

"I didn't say I knew anything. I never said I knew anything."

Nancy put her face in her hands and then looked up and said in a low voice, "What do I look like?"

"Terrible right now—it's very uneven. A good hair-dresser can shape it, though. There's a lot of hair left."

Nancy reached for her robe and put it on; she picked up the hair, held it for a moment, and then, with her usual practicality, still attractive, always attractive, dropped it into the wastebasket. She glanced around the room and said, "Well, let's clean up before he gets back, okay? And can you take me to the airport tomorrow?"

Lily nodded. They began to pick things up and put them gingerly away. When they had finished the bedroom, they turned out the light in there and began on the living room. It was difficult, Lily thought, to call it quits and go to bed. Kevin did not return. After a long silence Nancy said, "I don't suppose any of us are going to be friends after this." Lily shrugged, but really she didn't suppose so either. Nancy reached up and felt the ends of her hair, and said, "Ten years ago he wouldn't have done this to me."

Had it really been ten years that they'd all known one another? Lily looked around her apartment, virginal again, and she was frightened by it. She felt a sudden longing for Kevin so strong that it approached desire, not for Kevin as he was but for Kevin as he seemed—self-confident, muscular, smart. Her throat closed over, as if she were about to cry. Across the room Nancy picked up one of her hairbrushes with a sigh —and she was, after all, uninjured. Lily said, "Ten years ago he might have killed you."

Jeffrey, Believe Me

My fondness for you I set aside. That you have always attracted me I set aside. That I had gone seven weeks (since Harley, you will remember) without, even that I set aside. I swear to you, Jeffrey, my motives were altruistic to the last degree. Humanity was what I was thinking of. Humanity and, specifically, the gene pool.

I might, as you would perhaps suggest, have consulted you. Needless to say, I thought of it. But where? Over café mocha after dinner, inserted somehow into both our speculative glances at the waiter, do I lean across the table dripping necklaces into the dessert and say, "Let's make a baby, Jeffrey"? Do I risk having to retreat into my chair and endure rejection while tonguing *mousse au chocolat* off my gold chains? My mother once dipped her left breast into a wedding cake, and my father licked the half-moon of *crème au beurre* from her peach satin, but that is precisely the point, Jeffrey. We aren't on such familiar terms. I will clue you in, J., with no condescension but only respect for your separate but equal experience: one whispers "So-and-so, let's make a baby!" only in the most passionate or most boring of circumstances. One always means it, but never does it.

And, truthfully, by the time I was ready to consult you, I had made up my mind. You are a thoughtful man, even cautious. "But let's talk about it," you would have said. "Let's wait a bit." Perhaps then, "I think we'd better not." Mine is the necessary affectionate nature, and I have plenty of money. The internal logic, the organic growth of my plan could possibly have been distorted. I wanted it to be perfect. Persons are not created lightly. Who can tell the lifelong effect of a cacophonous conception?

I eventually decided against alcohol and in favor of marijuana. The point was not to incapacitate you, but confuse you. I admit I was foraging about among a pastiche of high school and college experiences reconsidered. You were right to sense something odd in my insistence that dinner could not be put off an evening, though I know you work on Tuesdays. But when one has to deal with thirty hours, calculated rhythmically and astrologically, one is not interfered with by the trivialities of custom. You arrived punctually, considerate as always, three-piece-suited as always, bringing, as always, a bottle of St.-Emilion, though I hadn't told you about the roast chicken. You were right to mistrust my mood. The tentatively seductive me you had not before seen, silk skirt and no underpants (mindful that we had once agreed on the aesthetic virtues of my buttocks), the knees never crossed, slipping unconsciously apart, the shirt unbuttoned between the breasts. All for my benefit, not yours. Indeed, you only subliminally noticed (we were discussing your mother, I believe, and you asked twice if somebody else was coming). How haltingly the conversation moved. I told you I was tired, unable to talk fluently, and you believed me. Actually, now that I had decided, had gone so far as to lay my snare in the brownies, I could not withhold my glance. I will never forget the pepper-and-salt trousers you wore, the way the material fanned away from each inseam and stretched smoothly around each thigh. Cuffs. Those pants had cuffs and you wore black socks with russet clocks and tan shoes.

Set aside your modesty and think carefully what sort of man you are. Review your life. Look in the mirror if need be. To begin with, forty long (a graceful size) and thick curly hair (indeed, ringlets). Look into your eyes, Jeffrey. In all honesty, how much bluer could they be? And how much thinner and more arched your nose? And disfigurement. Where are the large pores? Is there the thread of a varicose vein? I know you have never worn glasses, had a pimple, used an Ace bandage. Even the soles of your feet are warm, not shockingly cold (take it from me), in the middle of the night.

I wanted to hear about your new pipe, that calabash you got in the city. But though you carefully explained, I still don't know what meerschaum is. I just know how you take out your pipe and put it back in, how the tip of your tongue flicks out to lick the mouthpiece, how you bite down on it and draw back your lips to keep talking, how unconscious and competent you are in lighting the match and watching the bowl and sucking in the air. And you take it out and put it back in, out of your mouth and in. Why had we never talked about cherries and briers and clays and corncobs before?

Our aperitif conversation augured well, I thought. After pipes, you will remember, we moved on to the marriage of Eileen and Dave, her third, his second. I, the experienced one, derogated the institution and marveled at their attachment to it. You replied, "And if you can't create your own

life-style in the twentieth century, what consolation is there?"
I chattered about angst and apocalypse in the usual fashion.
How were you to know my visions of blue bootees with
pompoms, velvety baby necks, and minuscule toes? Nothing,
you seemed to have said—and, more important, no one—
is illegitimate at the latter end of human history.

Dinner was intended to relax you. I don't like beef
consommé, but I know you do, and you always want roast
capon for the wine; Caesar salad and fresh croutons, your
favorite, and infant peas sautéed with baby onions *aux fines
herbes,* mine; the usual bread; a fresh tangerine ice (home-
and hand-made, J., beaten every quarter hour all afternoon).
The brownies perhaps were a bit obvious, great slabs of chocolate lathered with icing, walnut pieces scattered through
like confetti, not a seed, not a stem, the dope ground into
marijuana flour and disguised by a double dose of double
Dutch. And then you said, "I can't."

"Maybe over coffee," gnashing my teeth at my own
vanity, my anxiety to impress you with my cooking, as if I
had wanted marriage rather than motherhood. In my lap I
held my hands because they wanted to touch you. You drank
coffee. Did you notice the Jersey cream? I said, "Want a
brownie?" I could tell by your smile that you wanted to
please me. "In a while. Have a cup of coffee with me. I'll
get it." And there was your round little butt passing sideways
between my chair and the coffee table, nearly brushing my
face. You would put a dollop of Kahlua in it, I seemed jumpy.
Oh that I had bitten your left bun right then. "Thank you."
Do you remember how demurely I said thank you, smoothing
the silk in my lap?

But Jeffrey, as adults we pretend that handsome is as
handsome does. Really, you have done handsomely. Music,

for example, is only your hobby, and yet you play three instruments. Everyone agrees you are a masterful raconteur, and yet a temperate man (that last, indeed, was the greatest obstacle to my plot). You have a graceful and generous mind. What was the last spiteful comment you made? There are none within my memory. Your minor virtues are countless: you leave proper tips, you hang up your clothes, you are not too proud to take buses. This is just living, you would say, and yet all those thank-you notes add up. Not wishing to embarrass you, I will drop the subject, adding only that we both know what a remarkable child you were and that you have been steadily successful.

When the coffee cup was heavy in my hands, you sat down on the table and looked at me. "I'm concerned for you," you said. I was flattered. When you leaned forward, you smelled like tobacco, wool, and skin. The bowls of your cobalt irises float well above the lower lids, and there is white in them like skeletons. I had never noticed that before. The pupils dilated. You do like me. It was time to take your face between my palms and gain your favors with one passionate, authoritative, skilled, yet vulnerable kiss. I said, "Harley is threatening to cut his throat again." I hadn't heard from Harley, but it's a threat he offers preferred women every few months.

"When did he call?"

"My mother is dying."

"Of what?"

"The police beat up my grandfather for passing out deaf-and-dumb cards."

"Both your grandfathers are dead."

"My sister anticipated a walk light, and a taxi ran over her feet."

"What did you do today?"

"I washed DDT off infant peas and baby onions. What do you think of babies, Jeffrey?"

"They're very flavorful." This game we play when I want to inform you tactfully that I am strong enough for the urban nightmare. Your concern must have been assuaged; you removed to a chair beyond the table. We talked about the granular universe, as I remember.

"Please have a brownie?" My offer perhaps seemed tiresome. For me, I knew you would. I did, too. They tasted indescribably musty. I wanted to say, "It's only the marijuana." You were too polite to mention it. You must have felt hungry, because you had another. Then another. I wanted to ask, "And why do you prefer men, Jeffrey?" but I merely said, "You smell good," and got up to clear the table. We had cleaned the chicken of every morsel of flesh. When I came back, you were asleep. Post nitrates, post Hitler, post strontium-90, I got a hand mirror out of my purse and held it before your nostrils. A healthy fog. Still, I was disappointed. You would indeed be staying the night, but in a near coma.

Woman, Jeffrey. Joy, by Jean Patou, a dollar a dab. Fragrant, smooth, rosy. Draped in fragrant (lavender), smooth (silk spun by the very worms themselves), and abundant tissues of robin's egg and full-bodied burgundy. Woman standing in a draft in her tawny stockings regarding her erect nipples with her brown but really yellow eyes, her black hair shifted shinily forward in the light, her clean clean clean face, every pore purged. Let me tell you, J., that I, too, have fallen asleep *in media seductione.* But good heavens, he was not only a freshman given to wearing an orange and black stocking cap to bed on football weekends; he had three splinted fingers and was there on a wrestling scholarship. I removed your shoes.

After finishing the dishes, dusting and wiping out the china cabinet, mopping the floors, washing the woodwork, replacing the light bulb in the front-hall closet and the one in the back pantry, Windexing the mirrors, sorting through all my makeup bottles and the medicine chest, and hemming up a new dress, I removed your jacket.

Frankly, Jeffrey, the building of model ships for nautical museums and private collections is nothing so much as honorable. You fashion every mahogany plank and rosewood mast, you overcast raw edges of sails, you braid the lines and lanyards, you tie the microscopic knots. Remember the time I nosed around your mullion-windowed shop?

"Of course I'll tell you."

"Is it with long tweezers, the way they do radium?"

The masts and sails nestled together on the deck like bat wings. You slid the hull gently, tightly, through the neck and positioned it on the floor of the bottle. "Pull this string." I pulled. The masts stood up and the sails spread and the bottle filled with wind. Won't you believe the lifelong importance of this mystery to me?

I disrobed. I brushed my teeth twice and flossed them. I plucked two hairs between my eyebrows. I washed my face with glycerine-rosewater soap. I brushed my hair a hundred strokes and poured peroxide into my ears and navel. I applied cups of water to my eyeballs. I gargled. I blew my nose. I emptied my bladder. I cleaned under my fingernails. I buttoned my cotton pajamas crotch to chin, then zipped myself into a turtleneck bathrobe and sat down on the bed. The only, though enormous, bed.

As if I had intended to all along, I walked up to you

in the living room, removed every stitch you had on, and threw it all down the air shaft in the hall. I was touched by the frayed waistband of your Munsingwears. When I came back you were shivering every so often, but still comatose. I turned up the heat and, for the time being, covered you with an antique quilt, rose of Sharon pattern, as one such as I, a woman, a cook, a believer in simple plants like yeast, might set the dough on to rise. I pulled on my mukluks, muffled my neck, and sat down with Roland Barthes.

But you (it) were (was) inescapable. Perfectly lubricated in your bendings and unbendings, eyes almost completely closed, with every manifestation of presence and yet gone, gone. I threw down the Barthes, yanked off the quilt, and took a good look. My eye, of course, flew at once to your penis for evidence of your inner life. But I dragged my gaze away. There wasn't much of you to see, mostly skin not unlike my own. I fingered some of it. It pinched up elastically, resumed its shape, changed white to red to pink. I laid my cheek, my breast, my shoulder, my knee on various parts of you, to tune you in over unusual receivers. I smelled you. You smell like hollandaise for some reason. Experimentally, I applied lips and tongue to your penis. It grew to a firm, tasteful size, unblemished, stem and cap nicely differentiated. I let it wilt. I am not a necrophiliac. Like all of us raised with the Scientific Method, simply curious. I said, still robed, pajamaed, slippered, and muffled, picking Roland B. up off the carpet and smoothing wrinkled pages, "Jeffrey! I'll put you to bed." The first voice in hours, all night. You answered promptly. "Watch your fingers."

"What?"

"Power drills are a dangerous business." Thus your inner life inexorably proceeded, not exclusive of these hands with which I stood you up, the sharp corner of the table around which I steered you, the toilet I placed you next to, but relegating all of our surroundings with no compromise. "Piss!" I ordered. "That's easier said than done," you said, already doing it, your eyes adamantly closed.

Man, unconscious, naked in my bathroom, warm skin in jeopardy of cold surfaces, porcelain and metallic. The fluorescent light whitening and fattening him, the muscles in his narrow bony feet (the little piggy that stayed home shorter than the one that went to market) tensing and relaxing as he loses and regains degrees of balance.

Your body. I guided it into the bedroom and got it up at the end of the bed. "Lie down, Jeffrey," I said, poking the small of its back. It toppled onto the bed, face down. I covered it up, pink sheet, red thermal blanket, white quilt, under its cheek, a down pillow. I hung up my own clothes, climbed into bed with it, turned out the light. Black shades, navy curtains, it was dark. I did, as you can imagine, kiss it on the cheek, laid an amicable hand on its scapula. I thought again of Einstein. I fell asleep, and woke up disoriented, fucking. "Where am I?" I said. In response, you came. But way of explanation, I added, "It's very dark." You simply said, "Mary." Truly that is my name, although the name of many. You used a very one-in-the-afternoon, fully conscious, what-shall-we-have-for-lunch sort of intonation. In the morning you were gone in a pair of my jeans and a sweat shirt.

It is January. I was glad to have kept your shoes. Since then, four weeks ago, where have you been? I do not accuse, I simply wish to know. That and where you intend to be, which will become increasingly important from now on.

Long
Distance

*K*irby Christianson is standing under the shower, fiddling with the hot-water spigot and thinking four apparently simultaneous thoughts: that there is never enough hot water in this apartment, that there was always plenty of hot water in Japan, that Mieko will be here in four days, and that he is unable to control Mieko's expectations of him in any way. The thoughts of Mieko are accompanied by a feeling of anxiety as strong as the sensation of the hot water, and he would like the water to flow through him and wash it away. He turns from the shower head and bends backward, so that the stream can pour over his face.

When he shuts off the shower, the phone is ringing. A sense that it has been ringing for a long time—can a mechanical noise have a quality of desperation?—propels him naked and dripping into the living room. He picks up the phone and his caller, as he has suspected, is Mieko. Perhaps he is psychic; perhaps this is only a coincidence; or perhaps no one else has called him in the past week or so.

The connection has a crystalline clarity that tricks him into not allowing for the satellite delay. He is already annoyed after the first hello. Mieko's voice is sharp, high, very Japanese, although she speaks superb English. He says, "Hello, Mieko," and he *sounds* annoyed, as if she calls him too much, although she has only called once to give him her airline information and once to change it. Uncannily attuned to the nuances of his voice, she says, "Oh, Kirby," and falls silent.

Now there will be a flurry of tedious apologies, on both sides. He is tempted to hang up on her, call her back, and blame his telephone—faulty American technology. But he can't be certain that she is at home. So he says, "Hello, Mieko? Hello, Mieko? Hello, Mieko?" more and more loudly, as if her voice were fading. His strategy works. She shouts, "Can you hear me, Kirby? I can hear you, Kirby."

He holds the phone away from his ear. He says, "That's better. Yes, I can hear you now."

"Kirby, I cannot come. I cannot go through with my plan. My father has lung cancer, we learned this morning."

He has never met the father, has seen the mother and the sister only from a distance, at a department store.

"Can you hear me, Kirby?"

"Yes, Mieko. I don't know what to say."

"You don't have to say anything. I have said to my mother that I am happy to stay with her. She is considerably relieved."

"Can you come later, in the spring?"

"My lie was that this Melville seminar I was supposed to attend would be offered just this one time, which was why I had to go now."

"I'm sorry."

"I know that I am only giving up pleasure. I know that my father might die."

As she says this, Kirby is looking out his front window at the snowy roof of the house across the street, and he understands at once from the hopeless tone of her voice that to give up the pleasure that Mieko has promised herself is harder than to die. He understands that in his whole life he has never given up a pleasure that he cherished as much as Mieko cherished this one. He understands that in a just universe the father would rather die alone than steal such a pleasure from his daughter. All these thoughts occur simultaneously and are accompanied by a lifting of the anxiety he felt in the shower. She isn't coming. She is never coming. He is off the hook. He says, "But it's hard for you to give it up, Mieko. It is for me, too. I'm sorry."

The sympathetic tones in his voice wreck her self-control, and she begins to weep. In the five months that Kirby knew Mieko in Japan, and in the calls between them since, she has never shed a tear, hardly ever let herself be caught in a low moment, but now she weeps with absolute abandon, in long, heaving sobs, saying, "Oh, oh, oh," every so often. Once, the sounds fade, as if she has put down the phone, but he does not dare hang up, does not even dare move the phone from one ear to the other. This attentive listening is what he owes to her grief, isn't it? If she had come and he had disappointed her, as he would have, this is how she would have wept in solitude after swallowing her disappointment in front of him. But this is her father's doing, not his. He can give her a little company after all. He presses the phone so hard to his ear that it hurts. The weeping goes on for a long time and he is afraid to speak and interfere with what will certainly be her only opportunity to give way to her feelings. She gives one final wailing "Ohhh" and then

73

begins to cough and choke. Finally she quiets, and then sighs. After a moment of silence, she says, "Kirby, you should not have listened."

"How could I hang up?"

"A Japanese man would have."

"You sound better, if you are back to comparing me with Japanese men."

"I am going to hang up now, Kirby. I am sorry not to come. Good-bye."

"Don't hang up."

"Good-bye."

"Mieko?"

"Good-bye, Kirby."

"Call me! Call me again!" He is not sure that she hears him. He looks at the phone and then puts it on the cradle.

Two hours later he is on the highway. This is, after all, two days before Christmas, and he is on his way to spend the holidays with his two brothers and their wives and children, whom he hasn't seen in years. He has thought little about this visit, beyond buying a few presents. Mieko's coming loomed, imposing and problematic. They had planned to drive out west together—she paid an extra fare so that she could land in Minneapolis and return from San Francisco— and he had looked forward to seeing the mountains again. They had made reservations on a bus that carries tourists into Yellowstone National Park in the winter, to look at the smoky geysers and the wildlife and the snow. The trip would have seemed very American to her. Buffalo and men in cowboy boots and hats. But it seemed very Japanese to him—deep snow, dark pines, sharp mountains.

The storm rolls in suddenly, the way it sometimes does on I-35 in Iowa, startling him out of every thought except alertness. Snow swirls everywhere, blotting out the road, the other cars, sometimes even his own front end. The white of his headlights reflects back at him, so that he seems to be driving into a wall. He can hardly force himself to maintain thirty-five miles an hour, although he knows he must. To stop would be to invite a rear-end collision. And the shoulder of the road is invisible. Only the white line, just beside the left front corner of the car, reveals itself intermittently as the wind blows the snow off the pavement. He ejects the tape he is playing and turns on the radio, to the state weather station. He notices that his hand is shaking. He could be killed. The utter blankness of the snowy whirl gives him a way of imagining what it would be like to be dead. He doesn't like the feeling.

He remembers reading two winters ago about an elderly woman whose son dropped her off at her apartment. She discovered that she had forgotten her key, and with the wind-chill factor at eighty below zero, she froze before she got to the manager's office. The winter before that a kid who broke his legs in a snowmobile accident crawled three miles to the nearest farmhouse, no gloves, only a feed cap on his head.

Twenty below, thirty below—the papers always make a big deal of the temperature. Including wind chill, seventy, a hundred below. Kirby carries a flashlight, a down sleeping bag, a sweat shirt that reads UNIVERSITY OF NEBRASKA, gloves and mittens. His car has new tires, front-wheel drive, and plenty of antifreeze. He has a thermos of coffee. But the horror stories roll through his mind anyway. A family without boots or mittens struggles two miles to a McDonald's through high winds, blowing snow, thirty below. *Why would they travel in that weather?* Kirby always thinks when he reads the papers, but of course they do. He does. Always has.

A gust takes the car, just for a second, and Kirby grips the wheel more tightly. The same gust twists the enveloping snow aloft and reveals the Clear Lake rest stop. Kirby is tempted to stop, tempted not to. He has, after all, never died before, and he has driven through worse than this. He passes the rest stop. Lots of cars are huddled there; but then, lots of cars are still on the highway. Maybe the storm is letting up.

As soon as he is past the rest stop, he thinks of Mieko, her weeping. She might never weep like that again, even if she heard of his death. The connection in her mind between the two of them, the connection that she allowed to stretch into the future despite all his admonitions and all her resolutions, is broken now. Her weeping was the sound of its breaking. And if he died here, in the next ten minutes, how would she learn of it? His brothers wouldn't contact her, not even if she were still coming, because they didn't know she had planned to come. And if she were ever to call him back, she would get only a disconnect message and would assume that he had moved. He can think of no way that she could hear of his death, even though no one would care more than she would. These thoughts fill him with self-pity, but at least they drive out the catalogue of horror: station wagon skids into bridge abutment, two people killed, two paralyzed from the neck down, mother survives unharmed, walks to nearby farmhouse. Kirby weighs the boredom and good fellowship he will encounter sitting out the storm at a truck stop against possible tragedy. Fewer cars are on the road, more are scattered on the median strip. Inertia carries him onward. He is almost to Minnesota, after all, where they really know how to take care of the roads. He will stop at the tourist center and ask about conditions.

But he drives past the tourist center by mistake, lost in thought. He decides to stop in Faribault. But by then the snow seems to be tapering off. Considering the distance he has traveled, Minneapolis isn't far now. He checks the odometer. Only fifty miles or so. An hour and a half away, at this speed. His mind eases over the numbers with customary superhighway confidence, but at once he imagines himself reduced to walking, walking in this storm, with only a flashlight, a thermos of coffee, a University of Nebraska sweat shirt—and the distance swells to infinity. Were he reduced to his own body, his own power, it might be too far to walk just to find a telephone.

For comfort he calls up images of Japan and southern China, something he often does. These images are the one tangible gift of his travels. So many human eyes have looked upon every scene there for so many eons that every sight has an arranged quality: a flowering branch in the foreground, a precipitous mountainside in the background, a small bridge between. A path, with two women in red kimonos, that winds up a hillside. A white room with pearly rice-paper walls and a futon on the mat-covered floor, branches of cherry blossoms in a vase in the corner. They seem like postcards, but they are scenes he has actually looked upon: on a three-day trip out of Hong Kong into southern China, with some other teachers from his school on a trip to Kyoto, and at Akira's house. Akira was a fellow teacher at his school who befriended him. His house had four rooms, two Japanese style and two Western style.

He remembers, of course, other scenes of Japan—acres

77

of buses, faces staring at his Westernness, the polite but bored rows of students in his classroom—when he is trying to decide whether to go back there. But these are not fixed, have no power; they are just memories, like memories of bars in Lincoln or the pig houses on his grandfather's farm.

And so, he survives the storm. He pulls into the driveway of Harold's new house, one he has not seen, though it is in a neighborhood he remembers from junior high school. The storm is over. Harold has his snowblower out and is making a path from the driveway to his front door. With the noise and because his back is turned, he is unaware of Kirby's arrival. Kirby stops the car, stretches, and looks at his watch. Seven hours for a four-hour trip. Kirby lifts his shoulders and rotates his head, but does not beep his horn just yet. The fact is that he has frightened himself with the blinding snow, the miles of slick and featureless landscape, thoughts of Japan, and the thousands and thousands of miles between here and there. His car might be a marble that has rolled, only by luck, into a safe corner. He presses his fingers against his eyes and stills his breathing.

Harold turns around, grins, and shuts off the snow-blower. It is a Harold identical to the Harold that Kirby has always known. Same bright snowflake ski hat, same bright ski clothing. Harold has spent his whole life skiing and ski-jumping. His bushy beard grows up to the hollows of his eyes, and when he leans into the car his mustache is, as always, crusted with ice.

"Hey!" he says. He backs away, and Kirby opens the car door.

"Made it!" Kirby says. That is all he will say about the

trip. The last thing he wants to do is start a discussion about near misses. Compared with some of Harold's near misses, this is nothing. In fact, near misses on the highway aren't worth mentioning unless a lot of damage has been done to the car. Kirby knows of near misses that Harold has never dared to describe to anyone besides him, because they show a pure stupidity that even Harold has the sense to be ashamed of.

At dinner, over sweet and savory Nordic fare that Kirby is used to but doesn't much like, the people around the table, his relatives, waver in the smoky candlelight, and Kirby imagines that he can feel the heat of the flames on his face. The other people at the table seem unfamiliar. Leanne, Harold's wife, he has seen only once, at their wedding. She is handsome and self-possessed-looking, but she sits at the corner of the table, like a guest in her own house. Eric sits at the head, and Mary Beth, his wife, jumps up and down to replenish the food. This assumption of primogeniture is a peculiarity of Eric's that has always annoyed Kirby, but even aside from that they have never gotten along. Eric does his best—earnest handshake and smile each time they meet, two newsy letters every year, pictures of the children (known between Harold and Kirby as "the little victims"). Eric has a Ph.D. from Columbia in American history, but he does not teach. He writes for a conservative think tank, articles that appear on the op-ed pages of newspapers and in the think tank's own publications. He specializes in "the family." Kirby and Harold have made countless jokes at Eric's expense. Kirby knows that more will be made this trip, if only in the form of conspiratorial looks, rolling eyes. Eric's hobby—Mary Beth's, too, for they share everything—is developing each nuance of his Norwegian heritage into a fully realized ostentation. Mary Beth is always busy, usually baking. That's all Kirby knows about her, and all he cares to know.

Across the table Anna, their older daughter, pale, blue-eyed, cool, seems to be staring at him, but Kirby can hardly see her. He is thinking about Mieko. Kirby looks at his watch. It is very early morning in Osaka. She is probably about to wake up. Her disappointment will have receded hardly a particle, will suck her down as soon as she thuds into consciousness. "Oh, oh, oh": he can hear her cries as clearly as if they were still vibrating in the air. He is amazed at having heard such a thing, and he looks carefully at the women around the table. Mieko would be too eager to please here, always looking after Mary Beth and Leanne, trying to divine how she might be helpful. Finally, Mary Beth would speak to her with just a hint of sharpness, and Mieko would be crushed. Her eyes would seek Kirby's for reassurance, and he would have none to give. She would be too little, smaller even than Anna, and her voice would be too high and quick. These thoughts give him such pain that he stares for relief at Kristin, Eric's youngest, age three, who is humming over her dinner. She is round-faced and paunchy, with dark hair cut straight across her forehead and straight around her collar. From time to time she and Leanne exchange merry glances.

Harold is beside him; that, at least, is familiar and good, and it touches Kirby with a pleasant sense of expectation, as if Harold, at any moment, might pass him a comic book or a stick of gum. In fact, Harold does pass him something—an icy cold beer, which cuts the sweetness of the food and seems to adjust all the figures around the table so that they stop wavering.

• • •

Of course his eyes open well before daylight, but he dares not move. He is sharing a room with Harold the younger, Eric's son, whose bed is between his and the door. He worries that if he gets up he will stumble around and crash into walls and wake Harold. The digits on the clock beside Harold's bed read 5:37, but when Kirby is quiet he can hear movement elsewhere in the house. When he closes his eyes the footsteps present themselves as a needle and thread, stitching a line through his thoughts. He has just been driving. His arms ache from gripping the wheel. The car slides diagonally across the road, toward the median. It slides and slides, through streams of cars, toward a familiar exit, the Marshalltown exit, off to the left, upward. His eyes open again. The door of the room is open, and Anna is looking in. After a moment she turns and goes away. It is 6:02. Sometime later Leanne passes with Isaac, the baby, in her arms.

Kirby cannot bear to get up and face his brothers and their families. As always, despair presents itself aesthetically. The image of Harold and Leanne's living room, matching plaid wing chairs and couch, a triple row of wooden pegs by the maple front door, seems to Kirby the image of the interior of a coffin. The idea of spending five years, ten years, a lifetime, with such furniture makes him gasp. But his own apartment, armchair facing the television, which sits on a spindly coffee table, is worse. Mary Beth and Eric's place, where he has been twice, is the worst, because it's pretentious; they have antique wooden trunks and high-backed benches painted blue with stenciled flowers in red and white. Everything, everything, they own is blue and white, or white with blue, and Nordic primitive. Now even the Japanese images he calls up are painful. The pearly white Japanese-style room in Akira's house was bitterly cold in the winter, and he spent one night there only half-sleeping, his thighs drawn to his chest, the perimeters of the bed too cold even to touch. His head throbbing, Kirby lies pinned to the bed by impossibility. He literally can't summon up a room, a stick of furniture, that he can bear to think of. Harold the younger rolls over and groans, turning his twelve-year-old face toward Kirby's. His mouth opens and he breathes noisily. It is 6:27.

At breakfast, Leanne sets a bowl of raisin bran before him, and he is struck by the elasticity of her motion. She smiles, so cool and kind that Kirby is suddenly daunted. Ten minutes later, when Anna enters the kitchen in her bathrobe, yawning, he recalls, suddenly, her appearance in the doorway to his room. Fifth grade. Only fifth grade. He can see that now, but the night before, and in the predawn darkness, she had seemed older, more threatening, the way girls get at fourteen and fifteen. "Cereal, sweetie?" Leanne says, and Anna nods, scratching. She sits down without a word and focuses on the back of the Cheerios box. Kirby decides that he was dreaming and puts the incident out of his mind; but, "sweetie"—he would like for Leanne to call him that.

Harold, of course, is at his store, managing the Christmas rush, and the house is less festive in his absence. Eric has sequestered himself in Leanne's sewing room, with his computer, and as soon as Anna stands up from breakfast, Mary Beth begins to arrange the day's kitchen schedule. Kirby rinses his cup and goes into the living room. It is nine in the morning, and the day stretches before him, empty. He walks through the plaid living room to the window, where he regards the outdoor thermometer. It reads four degrees below zero. Moments later it is five degrees below zero. Moments after that he is standing beside Harold's bar, pouring himself a glass of bourbon. He has already drunk it when

Anna appears in the doorway, dressed now, and staring at him again. She makes him think of Mieko again—though the child is blond and self-contained, she is Mieko's size. Last evening, when he was thinking of Mieko, he was looking at Anna. He says, attempting jovial warmth, "Good morning, Anna. Why do you keep staring at me?"

She is startled. "I don't. I was looking at the bookshelves."

"But you stared at me last night, at dinner. And you came to the door of my room early this morning. I know because I was awake."

"No, I didn't." But then she softens, and says with eager curiosity, "Are you a socialist?"

While Kirby is trying not to laugh, he hears Mary Beth sing from the kitchen. "Anna? Your brother is going sledding. You want to go?"

Anna turns away before Kirby can answer and mounts the stairs. A "No!" floats, glassy and definite, from the second floor.

Kirby sits down in one of the plaid armchairs and gazes at an arrangement of greenery and shiny red balls and candles that sits on a table behind the couch. He gazes and gazes, contemplating the notion of Eric and Mary Beth discussing his politics and his life. He is offended. He knows that if he were to get up and do something he would stop being offended, but he gets up only to pour himself another drink. It is nearly ten. Books are around everywhere, and Kirby picks one up.

People keep opening doors and coming in, having been elsewhere. Harold comes home for lunch, Leanne and Isaac return from the grocery store and the hardware store, Harold the younger stomps in, covered with snow from sledding, eats a sandwich, and stomps out again. Eric opens the study door, takes a turn through the house, goes back into the study again. He does this three times, each time failing to speak to Kirby, who is sitting quietly. Perhaps he does not see him. He is an old man, Kirby thinks, and his ass has spread considerably in the past four years; he is thirty-six going on fifty, round-shouldered, wearing slacks rather than jeans. What a jerk.

But then Kirby's bad mood twists into him, and he lets his head drop on the back of his chair. What is a man? Kirby thinks. What is a man, what is a man? It is someone, Eric would say, who votes, owns property, has a wife, worries. It is someone, Harold would say, who can chop wood all day and fuck all night, who can lift his twenty-five-pound son above his head on the palm of his hand.

After lunch the men have all vanished again, even Isaac, who is taking a nap. In various rooms the women do things. They make no noise. Harold's house is the house of a wealthy man, Kirby realizes. It is large enough to be silent and neat most of the time, the sort of house Kirby will never own. It is Harold and Eric who are alike now. Only Kirby's being does not extend past his fingertips and toes to family, real estate, reputation.

Sometime in the afternoon, when Kirby is still sitting quietly and his part of the room is shadowed by the movement of the sun to the other side of the house, Kristin comes in from the kitchen, goes straight to the sofa, pulls off one of the cushions, and begins to jump repeatedly from the cushion to the floor. When he says, "Kristin, what are you doing?" she is not startled. She says, "Jumping."

"Do you like to jump?"

She says, "It's a beautiful thing to do," in her matter-of-fact, deep, three-year-old voice. Kirby can't believe she knows what she is saying. She jumps three or four more times and then runs out again.

At dinner she is tired and tiresome. When Eric tells her to eat a bite of her meat (ham cooked with apricots), she looks him right in the face and says, "No."

"One bite," he says. "I mean it."

"No. I mean it." She looks up at him. He puts his napkin on the table and pushes back his chair. In a moment he has swept her through the doorway and up the stairs. She is screaming. A door slams and the screaming is muffled. When he comes down and seats himself, carefully laying his napkin over his slacks, Anna says, "It's her body."

The table quiets. Eric says, "What?"

"It's her body."

"What does that mean?"

"She should have control over her own body. Food. Other stuff. I don't know." She has started strong but weakens in the face of her father's glare. Eric inhales sharply, and Kirby cannot restrain himself. He says, "How can you disagree with that? It sounds self-evident to me."

"Does it? The child is three years old. How can she have control over her own body when she doesn't know anything about it? Does she go out without a coat if it's twenty below zero? Does she eat only cookies for three days? Does she wear a diaper until she's five? This is one of those phrases they are using these days. They all mean the same thing."

"What do they mean?" As Kirby speaks, Leanne and Mary Beth look up, no doubt wishing that he had a wife or a girl friend here to restrain him. Harold looks up, too. He is grinning.

Eric shifts in his chair, uncomfortable, Kirby suddenly realizes, at being predictably stuffy once again. Eric says, "It's Christmas. Let's enjoy it."

Harold says, "Principles are principles, any day of the year."

Eric takes the bait and lets himself say, "The family is constituted for a purpose, which is the sometimes difficult socialization of children. For a certain period of their lives others control them. In early childhood others control their bodies. They are taught to control themselves. Even Freud says that the young barbarian has to be taught to relinquish his feces, sometimes by force."

"Good Lord, Eric," Leanne says.

Eric is red in the face. "Authority is a principle I believe in." He looks around the table and then at Anna, openly angry that she has gotten him into this. Across Anna's face flits a look that Kirby has seen before, has seen on Mieko's face, a combination of self-doubt and resentment molded into composure.

"Patriarchy is what you mean," Kirby says, realizing from the tone of his own voice that rage has replaced sympathy and, moreover, is about to get the better of him.

"Why not? It works."

"For some people, at a great cost. Why should daughters be sacrificed to the whims of the father?" He should stop now. He doesn't. "Just because he put his dick somewhere once or twice." The result of too many bourbons too early in the day.

"In my opinion—" Eric seems not to notice the vulgarity, but Harold, beside Kirby, snorts with pleasure.

"I don't want to talk about this," Leanne says. Kirby blushes and falls silent, knowing that he has offended her.

It is one of those long holiday meals, and by the time they get up from the table, Kirby feels as if he has been sitting in a dim, candlelit corner most of his life.

There is another ritual—the Christmas Eve unwrapping of presents—and by that time Kirby realizes that he is actively intoxicated and had better watch his tone of voice and his movements. Anna hands out the gifts with a kind of rude bashfulness, and Kirby is surprised at the richness of the array: from Harold he has gotten a cotton turtleneck and a wool sweater, in bright, stylish colors; from Leanne a pair of very fancy gloves; from Isaac three pairs of Ragg wool socks; from Eric's family, as a group, a blue terry-cloth robe and sheepskin slippers. When they open his gifts, he is curious to see what the wrappings reveal: he has bought it all so long before. Almost everything is some gadget available in Japan but not yet in the States. Everyone peers and oohs and aahs. It gives Kirby a headache and a sense of his eyeballs expanding and contracting. Tomorrow night he will be on his way home again, and though he cannot bear to stay here, after all, he cannot bear to leave either.

He drifts toward the stairs, intending to go to bed, but Harold looms before him, grinning and commanding. "Your brain needs some oxygen, brother," he says. Then they are putting on their parkas, and then they are outside, in a cold so sharp that Kirby's nose, the only exposed part of him, stings. Harold strides down the driveway, slightly ahead of him, and Kirby expects him to speak, either for or against Eric, but he doesn't. He only walks. The deep snow is so solidly frozen that it squeaks beneath their boots. The only thing Harold says the whole time they are walking is, "Twenty-two below, not counting the wind chill. Feels good, doesn't it?"

"Feels dangerous," Kirby says.

"It is," Harold says.

The neighborhood is brightly decorated, and the colored lights have their effect on Kirby. For the first time in three Christmases he feels a touch of the mystery that he thinks of as the Christmas spirit. Or maybe it is love for Harold.

Back at the house, everyone has gone to bed except Leanne and Mary Beth, who are drying dishes and putting them away. They are also, Kirby realizes—after Harold strides through the kitchen and up the stairs—arguing, although with smiles and in polite tones. Kirby goes to a cabinet and lingers over getting himself a glass for milk. Mary Beth says, "Kristin will make the connection. She's old enough."

"I can't believe that."

"She saw all the presents being handed out and unwrapped. And Anna will certainly make the connection."

"Anna surely doesn't believe in Santa Claus anymore."

"Unofficially, probably not."

"It's Isaac's first Christmas," Leanne says. "He'll like all the wrappings."

"I wish you'd thought of that before you wrapped the family presents and his Santa presents in the same paper."

"That's a point, too. They're his presents. I don't think Kristin will notice them."

"If they're the only wrapped presents, she will. She notices everything."

Now Leanne turns and gazes at Mary Beth, her hands on her hips. A long silence follows. Leanne flicks a glance at Kirby, who pretends not to notice. Finally she says, "All right, Mary Beth. I'll unwrap them."

"Thank you," Mary Beth says. "I'll finish this, if you want." Kirby goes out of the kitchen and up to his bedroom.

The light is already off, and Harold the younger is on his back, snoring.

When he gets up an hour later, too drunk to sleep, Kirby sees Leanne arranging the last of Santa's gifts under the tree. She turns the flash of her glance upon him as he passes through the living room to the kitchen. "Mmm," he says, uncomfortable, "can't sleep."

"Want some cocoa? I always make some before I go to bed."

He stops. "Yeah. Why not? Am I mistaken, or have you been up since about six a.m.?"

"About that. But I'm always wired at midnight, no matter what."

He follows her into the kitchen, remembering now that they have never conversed and wishing that he had stayed in bed. He has drunk himself stupid. Whatever words he has in him have to be summoned from very far down. He sits at the table. After a minute he puts his chin in his hand. After a long, blank, rather pleasant time, the cocoa is before him, marshmallow and all. He looks at it. When Leanne speaks, Kirby is startled, as if he had forgotten that she was there.

"Tired?" she says.

"Too much to drink."

"I noticed."

"I don't have anything more to say about it."

"I'm not asking."

He takes a sip of his cocoa. He says, "Do you all see much of Eric and family?"

"They came last Christmas. He came by himself in the summer. To a conference on the future of the family."

"And so you have to put up with him, right?"

"Harold has a three-day limit. I don't care."

"I noticed you unwrapped all Isaac's presents."

She shrugs, picks at the sole of her boot. She yawns without covering her mouth, and then says, "Oh, I'm sorry." She smiles warmly, looking right at him. "I am crazy about Kristin. Crazy enough to not chance messing up Christmas for her."

"Today she told me that jumping off a cushion was a beautiful thing to do."

Leanne smiles. "Yesterday she said that it was wonderful of me to give her a napkin. You know, I don't agree with Eric about that body stuff. I think they naturally do what is healthy for them. Somebody did an experiment with one-year-olds, gave them a range of foods to choose from, and they always chose a balanced diet. They also want to be toilet trained sooner or later. I think it's weird the way Eric thinks that every little thing is learned rather than realized."

"That's a nice phrase." He turns his cup handle so that it points away and then back in his direction. Finally he says, "Can I tell you about something?"

"Sure."

"Yesterday a friend of mine called me from Japan, a woman, to say that she couldn't come visit me. Her father has cancer. She had planned to arrive here the day after tomorrow, and we were going to take a trip out west. It isn't important, exactly. I don't know."

Leanne is silent but attentive, picking at the sole of her boot. Now that he has mentioned it, the memory of Mieko's anguish returns to him like a glaring light or a thundering noise, so enormous that he is nearly robbed of the power to speak. He pushes it out. "She can't come now, ever. She probably won't ever call or write me again. And really, this has saved her. She had all sorts of expectations that I couldn't have . . . well, wouldn't have fulfilled, and if she had come she would have been permanently compromised."

"Did you have some kind of affair when you were there?"

"For a few months. She's very pretty. I think she's the prettiest woman I've ever seen. She teaches mathematics at the school where I was teaching. After I had been with Mieko for a few weeks, I realized that no one, maybe in her whole adult life, had asked her how she was, or had put his arm around her shoulders, or had taken care of her in any way. The slightest affection was like a drug she couldn't get enough of."

"What did you feel?"

"I liked her. I really did. I was happy to see her when she came by. But she longed for me more than I have ever longed for anything."

"You were glad to leave."

"I was glad to leave."

"So what's the problem?"

"When she called yesterday, she broke down completely. I listened. I thought it was the least I could do, but now I think that she is compromised. Japanese people are very private. It scares me how much I must have embarrassed her. I look back on the spring and the summer and yesterday's call, and I see that, one by one, I broke down every single one of her strengths, everything she had equipped herself with to live in a Japanese way. I was so careful for a year and a half. I didn't date Japanese women, and I was very distant—but then I was so lonely, and she was so pretty, and I thought, well, she's twenty-seven, and she lives in this sophisticated city, Osaka. But mostly I was lonely."

Leanne gazes across the table in that way of hers, calm

and considering. Finally she says, "Eric comes in for a lot of criticism around here. His style's all wrong, for one thing. And he drives Harold the younger and Anna crazy. But I've noticed something about him. He never tries to get something for nothing. I admire that."

Now Kirby looks around the room, at the plants on the windowsill, the hoarfrost on the windowpanes, the fluorescent light harsh on the stainless-steel sink, and it seems to him that all at once, now that he realizes it, his life and Mieko's have taken their final form. She is nearly too old to marry, and by the end of her father's cancer and his life she will be much too old. And himself. Himself. Leanne's cool remark has revealed his permanent smallness. He looks at his hands, first his knuckles, then his palms. He says, "It seems so dramatic to say that I will never get over this."

"Does it? To me it seems like saying that what people do is important." And though he looks at her intently, seeking some sort of pardon, she says nothing more, only picks at her boot for a moment or two, and then gets up and puts their cups in the sink. He follows her out of the kitchen, through the living room. She turns out all the lights, so that the house is utterly dark. At the bottom of the stairs, unable to see anything, he stumbles and puts his hand on her arm. She takes it, in a grasp that is dry and cool, and guides it to the banister. Then, soft and fleeting, he feels a disembodied kiss on his cheek.

Dynamite

I used to not call my mother or my brother and sister because their phones were being tapped, but then I just got out of the habit. Those calls were all the same. For one thing, the phone had to ring six or eight times before my mother would answer it. "What are you doing?" I would ask.

"I hate to talk about all of that trivia," she would say.

"What trivia?" This was a ploy.

"How people pass the hours, what they are cooking or eating, or have eaten."

Better begin with the basics, I thought. "What are you wearing?"

"Some clothes."

"That's promising, Mom. Do you look like a bag lady today?"

But it was impossible to get a rise out of her. "I don't know," she would say. "I don't think in those terms."

And then, "How are you, Mom?"

"I'm fine." We all said that. My sister, Miriam, was throwing herself away on Methedrine addicts; my brother, Avram, only left his room to take laundry to Mom's place, my mother had no activities she would admit to. When they asked me, I was fine, too, but I had the excuse of making bombs, something, I told myself, they didn't want to know. I didn't miss calling them for a long time, but now I remember our tones, how glad we were to hear from one another. I have had the urge to call, but I am still out of the habit, and I wonder if their phones are still being tapped.

My mother was sixty-eight yesterday. She was born on July 20, 1919, at nine in the morning. Last night I was out with my friend Michael, and he didn't know how old his mother was, or his father, even though he sees them every month or so. He does, however, know *how* they are. We were eating a pizza, and he said, "I don't believe my mother. She went bicycling with my sisters, and she tried to ride no hands and fell down and broke her wrist." He shook his head, and I nearly choked with envy, that he should be possessed of this little incident. He sent her a get-well card and a subscription to a magazine called *New Woman.*

I met Michael at work. We are shift engineers at a Farm Services fertilizer plant, glamourless jobs in the chemical engineering world. When the recruiter came to campus during the last semester of my M.S., eight years ago, I was the only one who signed up for an interview, and the only woman, to boot. They didn't look too deeply into my background. No security checks for "mud chemists." Michael's father and brother run a farm that's been in the family for a hundred years, up north, and his uncle has the Farm Services coop in their town. The apple doesn't fall far from the tree. From air and natural gas we make ammonia. The plant is seventeen years old, and what we do at work is check seams and tolerances and operational procedures, organize repair schedules, file reports about plant safety, and set an example of cleanliness, heed, and order for the production workers.

Ammonia is poisonous. It should never get into the air, but it does. What we chat about is how you might jell it into long, inert strips, strips that a farmer could lay like rope in his furrows, then disk under. Strips that would contain cow manure and diatomaceous earth and alfalfa flakes, a whole meal for the soil. You'd buy it by the roll, like Christmas ribbon. Or you could sell, not ammonia, but ammonia-producing bacteria. The farmer would buy it in bags and spread it over the soil in the fall. With the cover and moisture of snowfall, the bacteria would go to work, and by spring the soil would be ammoniated. What we argue about is why the production workers don't always follow safety procedures. This argument has moved into the realm of the personal and habitual. I always point out to Michael that he has the same complaint about his ex-wife and his children—they won't follow instructions. He says of me that relying on explanations rather than discipline ("Threats!" I say. "Just call it threats!") allows the workers too much leeway and is my refusal to take appropriate responsibility for things. There have been no accidents in six years and we have the best record of leak detection in the state. We make a good team.

My father was an exterminator. He started out in the thirties, shooting rats with a .22. He died when I was twelve. He left my mother money enough to make it just possible for her to do nothing at all. His name was Sidney Stein. When I left New York after the bombings, I changed my name to Alexandra Day. I am still known as Sandy, though. I used to be Jewish, and now I am not. I used to be a New Yorker, and now I am a Missourian. I used to live an urban life, and now I live in the country. I used to be a history and political science major at Barnard, and now I am a chemical engineer, and I don't open a book from one month to the next, unless it is some kind of manual. Michael started out as a theoretical physicist. He talks a lot about beauty. I don't see a lot of beauty around me. But I think that the world is a serviceable and solid place.

I could have told my grandfather about building bombs. His hero was Peter Kropotkin, the anarchist. For practical matters he accepted socialism, but the endless business of political meetings tormented him. He was an impatient man. When I was four, I picked all the tulips he had planted in front of his apartment in Brooklyn. I asked to have one; then, in a kind of greedy trance, I broke every crisp stem and made a bouquet. The tulips were pink and fragrant and I remember deliberately turning my back to him while I smelled them, then turning to face him. He was standing on the steps of the apartment building, and he looked down at me. He said, "You are a little capitalist, that you must have every one and leave nothing for the others?" Then he spit contemptuously into the areaway that led under the building to the trash cans. I didn't dare throw down the flowers, though they embarrassed me now, or depreciate them in any way. Without him telling me, I knew that his trip to the flower shop, his digging of the holes, his addition of the fertilizer, his setting of the bulbs was what I had taken all for myself. The labor theory of value. I also knew what a capitalist was. I thought everybody did.

How did Grandfather think of my father, who employed fifteen men and owned a building and seven trucks? I don't really know. It is all very long ago. Trivia. My grandfather would have said that the life of the individual is trivial indeed. He used to rail against Freud, against novels, against hospitals and doctors, against paying too much attention to what you ate, and against talking about yourself. Glorifying the one over the many, he called it. Although he railed against religion, they had a minyan at his apartment when my father died, and he said kaddish. It was one of my father's seven trucks that popped out of gear when he was standing behind it and pinned him against a wall, crushing him, and not quickly, to death. "Think! Do *not* work in restricted areas by yourself! Accidents *can* be avoided!" The apple doesn't fall far from the tree.

My mother, who two years from yesterday will be the age of my grandfather when he died an old man, was never Jewish. She was a singer with a jazz band during the Second World War. She had blond hair and sang with a guy who became Perry Como. She was from Asheville, North Carolina, and her mother and father had both died by the time she and the band got to New Jersey and New York. The story is very sketchy. It sounds to me now, as I think about it, that the trivia she didn't like to talk about was her life. My grandmother thought she was too tall, didn't know how to cook or dress, was eccentric. Our apartment was a mess. "So what does she do all day?" my grandmother would say. The eternal question. But they, and their cousins, were her only family. After my father died and then my grandfather, she lost touch with them, and had no one but Avie and Miriam and me. "Isn't there anyone at all down south, Mom?" I would say. "No cousins? Don't we have cousins down south?"

"There must be, somewhere," she would answer vaguely. "Everyone from around there is related."

. . .

Now I've been talking a lot about those days, as if they were more important than these days, or than the days since, but they weren't. For sheer happiness, things were best in Kansas. I lived with a guy for three years in a farmhouse on a hilltop. There was a windbreak of evergreens on the north side of the house, and the fields of wheat and sunflowers spread away for miles in every direction. I was studying Chem E., Scott was tending bar and playing in a band, we had three dogs and seven cats, and parties all the time. He had been to Vietnam and married, briefly. We agreed to forget the past, to make everything start all over. The oldest dog, a stray we got out of the pound, who was missing an ear and always snarled and snapped if you surprised him, was named Born Yesterday. We gardened and cooked and bought lots of records. We meditated twice a day and tried to overlook each other's unusual behaviors. After a while, to conceal the silence between us, we started talking about "wordless communion." That was the goal. It was soothing to think of. I liked my work. It got in everywhere—I would refer to the popcorn popper as a "popcorn containment building" or to the month of August as "zucchini detonation month" or our lovemaking as "the insertion of tab A into slot B." Desperate bad jokes that Scott perceived as put-downs. He was killed on his motorcycle.

I built more bombs than the FBI thinks I did. It's funny what reminds me of them—clocks, of course. Penny wrappers in banks, because they are about the same color as dynamite paper was. Once I was putting up a new closet rod, and as my fingers wrapped around it, I felt a frisson of breath-catching uncertainty—closet rod is about the diameter and density of a stick of dynamite. Sometimes I am overcome with the conviction that there is something dangerous in the basement that I must get rid of, though I can't think what it is.

When I offered my services in the movement, I had been hanging around meetings and saying smart things for about a year. I knew how to go out to Jersey and buy dynamite at farm equipment stores. I dared to have a number eight blasting cap in my pocket, a piece of bravado that would not tempt me now, and when one of them said, "How would you cause a lot of damage to Ma Bell?" I said, "Twenty-five sticks of dynamite in the center of the building, between a couple of elevator shafts. You'd probably get the electrical system, too." I pulled out the blasting cap and rolled it casually around my palm. He smiled. It was like a kiss. His name was Maury Nassiter, and he had a girl friend, a wispy Quaker. She thought he was exotic, but I had his number: he'd been raised about six blocks from my grandparents' old building, and his cousin knew my aunt Tova. He was the handsomest man I have ever seen. Maury had either lost his manners, or never had any, because he wasn't very nice to that pretty girl, whose name was Eileen Hobhouse, but he clung to her. He never made a pass at me, but I was special. I joked around. I tempted death. He treated me very respectfully, for a leftist.

I used to watch him with Eileen, instructing her. She would turn the crank on the ditto machine and he would say things like, "The important thing in a relationship is the struggle aspect," or "When the bosses have succeeded in forcing the worker to consume his own goods, then there's a crash, and that's the excuse for moving the means of production elsewhere. Do you see that?" Eileen would crank and nod. We ate communally. Maury would sit down to his bowl of rice and beans and hot sauce, and admire it for a moment, then say to Eileen, "Doesn't this make you feel connected to the whole Third World?" To me, he would say, "Can I get it all in my backpack?" and I would say, "Mark should take half and go by the PATH train." I heard that he bargained for a reduced charge, maybe in exchange for naming me, among others, but I was gone by that time, and Maury didn't know who I'd become or where I was. Neither did anyone else.

Last night Michael and I sat out in my garden. I think he was perplexed at how I kept questioning him about his mother. She drives a tractor, she has five daughters, she reads *The New York Review of Books*. He shifted around in his chair and said, "Stop looking at me like she's some kind of phenomenon! She's a woman who lives on a farm!" The images were wrong, which is why I kept asking for more. Nothing about her soothed me. Finally I said, "What does she cook? What's the *worst* thing she cooks?"

"Jesus," he said. Then he leaned back in his chair and looked out into space. After a few minutes, he said, in a deep, and I think unconscious, voice, "The wheeling stars." I smiled. I was crawling around between the rows in the garden, hands and knees, and slapping the dirt, just to feel the resistant give of the soil. The solidity of the earth was something I hadn't experienced before I came here. Now I don't know if I would rather see it from a distance—its curve and spread—or feel it, or smell it. There are people who eat it, I've heard. So I crawl around the garden, then I stand up and inhale and look, then I crawl around again. "I'm sorry," Michael said. "What are you doing?"

"Pulling weeds," I said. That was sufficient. To a farm kid, pulling weeds is always an acceptable, and even ennobling, activity.

He didn't leave until one. Listening to Michael talk about his mother made mine seem very present, so present that to have picked up the receiver and dialed the numbers, to have overlooked the passage of fifteen years, seemed easy. But in New York it was already after two, and I didn't have the first notion about where she was, or where Miriam and Avram were, or even whether they were still alive. I suppose that they know that I am still alive, by the presence of my face on every post office wall in the country, but maybe they don't. Those displays have a way of going out of currency. Or if I died, or were captured, maybe it would get on the local news in New York. Others have. But they all stuck to the east coast or the west coast, went underground, tried again. I'm the only one who just left, who got to the dead center of the continent. Here's something: when Kansas State sent for the transcript of my first two years of college, it just came. I explained the name change by alluding to a failed marriage, I searched my adviser's face for some clue I had been discovered, I planned my getaway (to South Dakota). He nodded, the FBI never appeared, and I unpacked.

Well, I didn't call my brother, then my sister, then my mother. I think that resurrection should be prepared for rather carefully. I don't mean mine. They can't prepare for mine. I mean theirs. I'm not sure that I could bear it, bringing them to life again.

I do long, with a sort of physical itch, to tease my mother, to sit at the dinner table, aghast at what she has put before us, and say, "Mom! This is slop! What is this? Don't you go into D'Agostino's by the front door, with the customers?" My brother would be laughing. My sister would be laughing. My mother would lift her fork with dignity, and say, "It's fine, it's good. You children are so persnickety."

Those dynamite operations manuals were the first manuals I ever looked into, and I loved the flatness of the prose, the elementary school drawings. And that is where my life began. The fact is that I am a happy person. Now that I know the lingo, I might call those banks and supply depots "randomly selected containment buildings" and the explosions themselves "very sudden chemical reactions." Maybe one of my bombs did kill someone, maybe one did, though none of the newspaper accounts ever reported such a thing, and the wanted poster doesn't mention a death. All of them went off after midnight, or in deserted military installations. But I often wonder, what if someone died? I look around my kitchen, out at the garden, down the hall at the oval glass in the front door. I feel the love that I feel every day for the simple objects of this solitude, for the spacious silence mid-continent, and I think, that's one price to pay for this, that life for this one. In college I would have been ashamed to think such a thought, but now, every day, with every safety check, every cost-benefit analysis, every decision about what maintenance to order first, I consider the comparative value of life, money, and time. I glorify the one over the many, this one over that one. Sometimes I look at my twenty-year-old face on the post office wall and wonder about that blank expression. Maybe it was terror, the terror of only being able to imagine what I had already known. Missouri is a place I could not have imagined if I hadn't been forced to.

· · ·

After Scott died, I did not know what to do with the dogs
or the cats, or the weeds in the garden, or the produce from
the garden. I did not know how to cook myself dinner or
check the oil in the truck we had bought together, or how
to answer the door if an unexpected knock came. At the time,
I thought that I was not especially sad, not sad enough,
maybe. But I see now that it is the ultimate sadness for a
smart person to become stupid, for a competent person to
wring her hands, for a person full of thoughts to go blank.
In the summer I fell into the well. When I was building
bombs I was never inattentive for a moment, but I sometimes
think about the well accident, wondering about how I could
have gotten so careless. I was standing in front of the pump,
filling a jug, and the well cover broke away beneath me. I
threw out my arms and caught myself at ground level. I
looked down at the surface of the water, some twelve feet
below. It was July 20, my mother's fifty-ninth birthday.
That was what I thought of as I clambered out of the well.
I began shivering uncontrollably in the middle of the night,
and shivered for five hours, because if I hadn't caught myself,
I would have treaded water until I died of exhaustion.

Last night, Michael brought an expensive bottle of wine for
dinner that he had gotten in Kansas City, and I served home-
made cannelloni. The pine nuts alone cost me eight dollars
a pound. We didn't have much to say to one another. When
the wine bottle was about a third full, Michael picked it up
to refill our glasses, but instead of pouring anything out, he
blew across the rim of the bottle. Then he poured some in
his glass and blew across it again. I find this sort of thing

tedious, so I held my hand out with a put-upon air. He poured some into my glass. I made a face. He blew again, and said, "Wait a minute."

"For what?"

"An idea."

"Personal or professional?"

He blew again, then he said, "Don't you have an old recorder or something around here?"

"It's on the mantel." He brought it to the table and began blowing into it, covering holes. Then he handed it to me and said, "Play a note."

I played a G.

"Hmm."

"What's the idea?"

"Why couldn't you tell whether there was a leak in a pipeline by the pitch of sounds going through it?"

"You mean the ammonia pipeline?"

"Or natural gas. Any pipeline. Blow another note. Put all your fingers down and lift one finger off at a time."

I played C, D, F, on up the instrument. He said, "You could even tell where it was, if you had the proper acoustic equipment."

"And you wouldn't have to turn off the pipeline to locate it, only to fix it. The pitch would locate it." I sat up and smiled. This was why Michael and I were together. "And you wouldn't have to send any special sound through it. In fact, you could test it regularly with just the pumping noise as your sound. You could rig up a computer program that would test it automatically, every thirty seconds."

"What if it were a branching pipe?"

"The branch would act as another leak. It would just change the base line pitch."

"Maybe." He poured out the wine and pushed back the food. I reached over to the sideboard for some graph paper. "Shit," he said, "I wish I remembered more acoustics."

"You're a genius," I said.

By midnight we had worked out all the variables we might find in the pipes at our own plant—multiple branching, length, diameter, acoustic interference, where to attach the sound-testing machines, how often to test, how many people would be put out of work (my contribution), how long production had been shut down for leak detection in the last year (Michael's contribution). By midnight, Michael was sitting very close to me on the couch, his shoulder against mine and his thigh along my thigh. When he finished his peach pie, I got up and carried his dish into the kitchen, and when I came back, I saw him. He has long legs, and he was sitting deep in the couch, so his knees jutted out above the coffee table. His blue jeans stretched around his thighs so that I could make out the hardness of the muscles. He scratched his full head of hair and pressed his beard down with the flat of his hand, the way he does. He is a good specimen. I like him to be a little distracted, and he was, so I sat down beside him again.

He squeezed me around the shoulders, and I looked around the room. The walls are a sort of rosy gray, the shades are Japanese rice paper. Hardwood floors, Scandinavian throw rugs, things my mother wouldn't have spent her money on. I love this room, the circles of light spreading and joining, the neatness and quietness of it, the fact that it is mine, and the doors are closed and locked and the shades are drawn. Michael said, in a voice that showed that he thought he had earned something by the ingenuity of his idea, "Talk to me. Let's have some news of your inner life."

I leaned against his knee and said, "I've told you that I don't have an inner life. There is no inner life." I kissed him. "I may look pretty, but it's just natural chemical engineering."

He smiled and said, "Reactor design, huh? Ever heard of sympathetic detonation?"

I smiled, and said, "That's purely a problem of distance." His flesh gave off a steady warm glow. I could not resist sliding my arms beneath his and laying my head against his chest.

After Michael left, I sat down to write my mother a letter. I addressed the envelope first, just to try it out. There is no reason at all to believe that she still lives where she did. She likes to move. She doesn't decorate, and she arranges the furniture the way it was in the previous apartment, but she does like the rooms to have different sizes and floor plans. We used to hate this moving habit of hers. Miriam would say, "Mom! We just got settled." I would say, "Mom, the landlord hasn't even managed to lose the deposit in the stock market yet!" and Avie would say, "Mom! What could be worse than this place? Let's stop here and not tempt our luck!"

But my mother would sigh and look around and say, "I just feel like I've lived this one out. It's too familiar. When I look at the dado on that wall, I get depressed."

"That's because it's dirty and needs painting! Let's just paint it another color. Avie and I will do it."

"If you spend money on a rented place, it's just thrown away."

"If you leave before the lease is up, it's thrown away, too."

"But that money's already gone. No one's counting on it. There are a lot of nice neighborhoods in Brooklyn that we've never tried."

Then Avie would say, "You can't live all those lives, Mom. You can only live one life." His voice would get patient and slow. "You want to move all the time because you want to try out other lives, but you can't."

"I don't know what you're talking about, Avram. I just don't like the space to be the same shape all the time."

"Why not? Why not?" He was angry.

"I don't know, Avram. People are different. They should accept people's differences."

I wrote "Dear Mom," then "Hi, Mom," then "Dearest Mom," then "Hey, Mom!" all in a row, on the same sheet of paper. The fact is, I have never written my mother a letter. I had never lived out of local calling distance before the bombings. I left the piece of paper next to the envelope on the kitchen table. I found a stamp and put it on the envelope, then I turned out the light and went to bed.

Once, Scott and I were having breakfast. He was looking at me, and then his eyes shifted and looked past me, out the window. All of a sudden, he jumped up and ran out the back door, grabbed the .22 on the back porch, and came around past the window. At the corner of the house, he dropped to one knee and let off a shot. Then he went out into the garden and came back with the rabbit that had been eating our lettuce plants. It was dead. He was proud of the shot, proud of its quick wit, I see now. Then, I just kept saying, "It was loaded? That gun was loaded? There was a loaded gun on our porch? I can't believe there was a loaded gun on our back porch!" When I remember that, I remember the shrillness of my voice. Finally he shouted, "Goddammit, would you go to school?" After the accident, I found that gun. He had loaded it again. I don't know why. He didn't hunt, even rabbits. Mutual silence got to be a position with us, something to be defended.

I couldn't sleep. Michael's idea was brilliant, a concrete example of how well we work together. He isn't very practical, and I could already see how he would get discouraged about the logistics of testing it without me. With the memory of his flesh against mine, the sense of our parallel tracks beginning to converge toward the horizon didn't entirely displease me.

At dawn, I was wide awake and itching to work in the garden. "The back forty," as Michael calls it, occupies the crown of a south-sloping hill, and I want to begin building terraced beds in the fall, perennial flowers and herbs, walls about four railroad ties high. If you stand far enough away, you will see a triangle of daffodils spreading down the hillside, then, later, a mass of red climbing roses growing over the terrace walls. As a rule, I live much more in the future than in the past. I crawled around the garden, clearing mulch from the paths and smelling the dewy odor of tomatoes and nasturtiums. I have only had one tomato so far this year, and no peppers. The vines are loaded, though. I crawled along next to the onions, and bent the tops down one by one. When I got up to go inside, it must have been about seven, and I was surprised to see a car pulling into the driveway. It was a late-model American sedan, dark blue. I followed my habit, which now doesn't have much to do with fear, and hid behind the bushes of tomato vines in their cages. The driver's door opened first, and a thick man in a sport shirt got out. He craned his neck toward the house, then wiped the back of his hand across his mouth. He didn't come out from behind the door, but stood, staring, then said, "Well, I don't know." Now the other door opened, and the gray head of an older woman rose above the roof of the car. She closed the door and walked toward my front steps. She had had her hair done, and she carried a very large purse pressed against her stomach, both hands gripping the clasp. She went up the steps and knocked, then, after a minute, peered in the window. She turned. "Doesn't seem to be anyone home."

The man said, "Truck's here."

"Is this the place, you think?"

"No telling. Want to look around?"

"Ought not, I don't think."

Nothing was recognizable about this couple. There was no one in my family who could have been transformed by any amount of time into either of them. Of the license plate, I could only see that it was out of state, white. The woman stood on the porch, her back to the door. She sighed, clicked the clasp of her purse. He said, "Come on, then." I didn't want to look at them any more, and so I lay down among the vines and listened for the departing crunch of their wheels. It came soon enough.

At ten o'clock I staggered into bed, exhausted at last. I woke up in the middle of the afternoon, disoriented and with the sound of the television in my ears, which frightened me. The sense of someone else in the house when I am waking up always frightens me. I always imagine that it is the FBI, making themselves at home, looking at my stuff, eating my food. I know that they don't do this, that in fact it was my fellow leftists who always did this back in the old days, but it is not rational, of course. Scott used to wake up shouting if one of the cats got under the covers. He thought it was a rat, and that he was in Khe Sanh again. Sometimes if thunderstorms began while we were sleeping, he would wake himself all the way up and listen to make sure that no whistles preceded the booms. War wounds. Now I realized that Michael was watching the baseball game in the living room, and I relaxed in bed and looked out the window.

If I had broken up with Scott and he had moved away, I would now be able to call him on the phone from time to time and ask him how he is. This is literally my only conscious wish. He would be smoking a cigarette, and he would inhale audibly, and I would imagine him taking his mustache between his lip and his lower teeth, biting it a little. Then he would say, "Sandy." We would be uncomfortable, too ready to prove, by talking fast, that we were both fine, happy, and productive, that we didn't miss each other. He might have a wife to show me up with, and kids. I would be exactly as I am now, turning over in this very bed, reaching for this very telephone. No molecule of the scene I am looking at now would be different, except that Scott would exist somewhere. The more that Michael comes around, the more I have this wish, the more I let myself indulge the fantasy of it, of saying, "Did we love each other? Did I love you?"

It is the third inning, and Michael is pounding the couch as I come into the room. An error at second, the Cardinals. Herr makes it, dropping the ball right out of his glove. "Shit!" yells Michael. "Did you see that dumb fucker?" His eyes follow me across the room. He says, "Do you mind that I'm here?"

"I told you you could come over, didn't I?"

"I didn't want to wake you."

"It's okay."

"What's the matter?"

"Nothing. I'm fine."

He doesn't say anything to this, turns his eyes back to the game. He is hurt by my manner. He says, "When I saw you were sleeping, I knew I should just go home."

"Don't, Michael. It's my fault. I was up at dawn, and now I feel really terrible."

"Why were you up at dawn?"

"Don't quiz me."

"I'm not quizzing you. I'm just asking." He stands up and goes over and turns off the television.

"Are we having a fight? You know I hate fighting."

He says, "I don't think we're having anything as promising as a fight." He goes toward the screen door and opens it. I am distracted by the color of the grass as the late afternoon sun falls across it, a hot, stark summer green, the way it gets only here, mid-continent. I turn my eyes to his face consciously, and he says, "You were so relaxed last night."

"I wasn't relaxed." He waits for me to say what I was, but I can't go on. And those are the last words we speak. He goes out to his car, gets in, and drives out of the driveway, pulling a tail of fine dust, and I go into the silent house. I sit on the couch where he was sitting.

My grandfather watched the Yankees on television every Saturday. My grandmother was under five feet, my grandfather not much over. My grandmother would be knitting an intricate and brightly colored outfit for one of those plastic dolls they had before Barbie dolls. This was for me. I hated dolls, and I would be pretending not to notice. Ringing through the apartment was the sound, not of the Yankees' announcer, but of *Rigoletto*, because part of watching the Yankees was turning the sound off and listening to the Texaco opera broadcast. My grandfather called himself a "Yankee," Yiddish pronunciation, "Yahnkih." The afternoons were long, and I was thinking, always, about something else, half bored, looking at the dust motes in the sunbeams, running my eyes across the titles in the bookcase and making objects of the long words. An opera is actually just about as long as a baseball game. I close my eyes now, and I look at my grandfather in his chair. He has thick hair, mink-brown, and his ears jut out of it like sails. His foot is up on a cushion, because he has gout in his big toe. He glances from the game to my grandmother and smiles. She is not looking at him. A socialist, an American, a Yahnkih, a man happy in his self-contradiction. I open my eyes, and I am in Missouri, and everything is collecting in my head, light and heavy, animate and motionless, bright and dark. Of my life it could truly be said that all is lost, except these things.

I remember when I first had the idea of making bombs. That is, I don't remember the circumstances, but I remember the feeling. I remember putting my hands out, palms curved and facing each other, about eight inches apart, as if a bomb, a hard small object, as I thought before I had seen any dynamite, could appear between them, if the force of desire alone could have that effect. Making a bomb was the most extreme thing I could think of to do, and once I had thought of it, I could not settle for anything less. All through the research, all through the dropping of hints, all through the wooing of Maury Nassiter, I was lusty and restless, the way I feel now.

It is the itch to do the most unthought-of thing, the itch to destroy what is made—the firm shape of my life, whether unhappy, as it was, or happy, as it is now.

But if I turn the imagined object and look at the other side, my motives are trivial, unimportant. My grandfather would say that what is true was what compelled me to act. He used to say, "When these bosses make you go faster until you can't keep up and they fire you to hire a younger man for less, you think this is by mistake?" He would say, "Of course they shoot me if I throw a stone through the window. You think that a pane of glass is not worth more than I am worth? Did the pane of glass cost more than the bullet? That's what they say to themselves." And every time he devalued himself, I got angry. It is an explosive pressure in my chest and shoulders that pulsates, I realize now, in time to my quickened breathing. It only takes a second to feel it again, to know again what my grandfather knew. I push myself out of the couch and walk to the front door. It is locked, and I open it and step out onto the porch, still panting. Since no one ever comes here, and Michael and I always park in the back, I know that this matted grass is from the morning, from the old couple. I stand looking at the tracks. Who could they be, that couple, other than the representatives of blame? I am struck, in retrospect, by their half-defeated air, the way the man stayed behind the car door, and the woman held her handbag in front of herself like a shield. Although it is certain they have nothing to do with me, my anger passes suddenly into remorse, the way the blossom of an explosion turns from yellow to orange, even as its shape billows outward. And the blast wave, though slower, is more punishing: the conviction that I might have understood more, acted less ruthlessly.

• • •

"I can't believe you ate it," says Avie.

"I ate it. What was wrong with it? I didn't want it to go to waste."

"Mom, it was rancid. You can't keep dressed salad in the refrigerator for a week and then eat it."

"Did it hurt me? Am I still standing here? Did I like it?"

"I can't believe you liked it."

"I don't like to waste things, that's what I don't like. It hurts me to waste things. Look at your socks."

Avie looks down at his socks, perplexed.

"Are there shoes on your feet?"

Avie sighs. "No."

"I can see those socks getting threadbare as I stand here."

"Mom, you have to think more of yourself. You have to value your own mouth, your own taste buds."

"You have to think more of your socks." She turns and walks out of the room.

He shouts after her, "Why are you this way?" But she doesn't bother to answer. Miriam goes over and puts her arm around his thin waist. We tease our mother, we question her, we watch her, but every time, she defeats us. There is no way in. Now she is in the other room. What is she doing? There are noises, a thump, a rustle. But when I go to look, she has gone into the bathroom and shut the door. I am filled with longing and curiosity.

Now I open my eyes again upon the Sunday summer afternoon, and I stand up from the couch and stretch. I move around the room, straightening, and into the bedroom, where I open the drawers and take out some underwear. I go to the closet and take out a bag and begin throwing things into it.

It is about three thirty. I have no plan. I will take each stage as it comes—south to I-70, north somewhere in Ohio to I-80. I will drive across the George Washington Bridge stealthily, press myself into the city as into jungle: not, as people think, to avoid capture, but rather to ambush my mother in some act, any act, to see her as she has never been seen before.

The
Age
of
Grief

D ana was the only woman in our freshman dental class, one of two that year in the whole dental school. The next year things changed, and a fifth of them were women, so maybe Professor Perl, who taught freshman biochemistry, didn't persist in his habit of turning to the only woman in the class and saying, "Miss McManus, did you understand that?" assuming that if Dana got it, so had everyone else (male). In fact, Dana majored in biochemistry, and so her predictable nod of understanding was a betrayal to us all, and our class got the reputation among the faculty of being especially poor in biochemistry, a statistical anomaly, guys flunking out who would have passed any other year. Of course, Perl never blamed himself.

Dentists' offices are very neat, and dentists are always washing their hands, and so their hands are cool and white and right under the nose, to be smelled. People would be offended if dentists weren't as clean as possible, but they hold it against us. On television they always make us out to be prissy and compulsive. If a murder has been committed and a dentist is in the show, he will certainly have done it, and he will probably have lived with his mother well into his thirties, to boot. Actors who play dentists blink a lot.

Dentists on television never have people coming in like the man who came to me today. His teeth were hurting him over the weekend, and so he went out to his toolbox and found a pliers and began to pull them all out, with only some whiskey to kill the pain. Pulling teeth takes a lot of strength and a certain finesse, one of which the man had and the other of which he lacked. What drove him into my office today, after fifteen years away from the dentist, was twenty-four broken teeth, some in fragments below the gum line, some merely smashed around the crown. Teeth are important. Eskimo cultures used to abandon their old folks in the snow when their teeth went, no matter how good their health was otherwise. People in our culture have a lot of privileges. One of them is having no teeth.

Dana was terrifically enthusiastic about dental school, or maybe the word is "defiant." When she came into the lecture hall every day she would pause and look around the room, at all the guys, daring them to dismiss her, daring them, in fact, to have any thoughts about her at all. To me, dental school seemed more like a very large meal that I had to eat all by myself. The dishes were arrayed before me, and so I took my spoon and went at it as deliberately as possible, chewing up biochemistry and physiology, then fixed prosthodontics and operative dentistry, then periodontics and anesthesia and pain control.

I was happy during lab, when we were let loose on the patients. They would file in and sit down in the rows of chairs; then they would lie back, and we would stretch these wire-and-rubber frameworks over their mouths. They were called rubber dams. You lodged the wires in the patient's mouth and then pulled the affected tooth through a tight hole in the rubber sheet. Our professors said that they made the tooth easier to see and get at. Really, I think, they were meant to keep the students from dropping something, a tooth or even an instrument, down that open throat. They also kept the patients quiet. That little barrier let them know that they didn't have to talk. Patients feel as if they ought to make conversation. Anyway, that huge hall would hush, and you would simply concentrate on that white tooth against that dark rubber, and the time would fly. That was the last time that I felt I could really meditate over my work. For a dentist, the social nature of the situation is the hardest thing.

I did well in dental school, but it seemed to me that I deserved more drama in my life, especially after I quit the building crew I had worked on every summer since I was sixteen. I quit the crew because I was making $4 an hour and one day I nearly crushed my left hand trying to lift a bunch of loose two-by-fours. It hurt, but before I even felt the pain (your neurons, if you're tall, take a while) I remembered the exact cost of my first year of dental school, which was $8,792.38. A lot of hours at $4 an hour.

I took on Dana. I felt about her the way she felt about dental school. I dared her to dismiss me, and I was determined to scare the pants off her. I took the front basket off my bike, and then I would make her sit on the handlebars at midnight while we coasted down the longest, steepest street in town. We did it over and over, eight nights in a row once. I figured the more likely outcome, death, was cheaper in the end than just wrecking my hands. Besides, it was like falling in love with Dana. I couldn't stop doing it and I was afraid she could.

After that, we'd go back to her place and make love

until the adrenaline in our systems had broken down. Sometimes that was a long time. But we were up at six, fresh and
sexy, Dana pumped up for the daily challenge of crushing
the dental school between her two fists like a beer can, and
me for the daily challenge of Dana. Now we have three
daughters. We strap them in the car and jerk the belts to
test them. One of us walks the older ones to school every
day, although the distance is two blocks. The oldest, Lizzie,
would be floored by the knowledge that Dana and I haven't
always crept fearfully from potential accident to potential
accident the way we do now.

If Dana were reminded these days that she hadn't graduated first in our class but third, she would pretend indif-
ference, but she was furious then. What did it matter that
Phil Levine, who was first, hadn't been out of his apartment
after dark in three years and his wife seemed to have taken
a vow of silence, which she broke only when she told him
she was going to live with another guy? Or that Marty Crockett, number two, was a certified genius and headed for NASA
as the first dentist in space? The result of her fury was an
enormous loan, for office, house, equipment, everything the
best, the most tasteful, the most up-to-date, for our joint
office and our new joint practice. We had been intending to
join two separate and established practices, etc., etc., the
conservative path to prosperity. Another result of her fury
was that the loan officer and his secretary were our first
patients, then his wife, her five children, one of her cousins.
The secretary has proved, in fact, an inexhaustible fount of
new patients, since she is related to everyone in three counties
and she calls them all regularly on the bank's WATS line. I
root-canaled three of her teeth last year alone.

Anyway, we dropped without pause from the drama of

Dana's four-point grade average into the drama of a $2,500 mortgage payment in a town where we knew no one and that already had four dental clinics. Dana put our picture in the paper, "Dr. David Hurst and Dr. Dana Hurst, opening their new clinic on Front Street." I was handsome, she was pretty, people weren't accustomed to going to good-looking dentists, she said. They would like it. Our office was next to the fanciest restaurant in town, far from Orthodontia Row, as Dana called it. It wasn't easy, and some of those huge mortgage checks were real victories of accounting procedure. As soon as it got easy, just a little easy, Dana got pregnant with Lizzie.

Dana likes being pregnant, even though, or because, each of our fetuses has negotiated a successful but harrowing path through early bleeding, threatened miscarriage, threatened breech presentation, and long labor. She likes knowing, perhaps, that when Dr. Dana Hurst comes through the obstetrician's door with the news that she is pregnant, the man had better get out his best machines and give his assistants a little extra training, because it isn't going to be easy, and wasn't meant to be.

Then there was the drama of motherhood—babies in the office, nursing between appointments, baby-sitter interviews that went on for hours while Dana probed into the deepest corners of the candidate's psyche, breasts that gushed in front of the dourest, least maternal patients. Assistants with twins. Those were the only kind she would hire for a while, just, I thought, to raise even higher the possibility that we wouldn't make it through the morning, through the week, through our marriage. I used to meditate over my patients in the dental school, but it wasn't enough. I wanted to be a dentist and have drama, too.

Now the children are all in school, or at least off the breast, we are prosperous and established on a semi—part-time schedule, and all Dana has to do is dentistry. Little machines. Itsy-bitsy pieces of cotton. Fragments of gold you can't pick up with your fingers. I think she thought it would get bigger, like Cinerama, and instead it gets smaller and smaller.

If she were writing this, she would say that I was an exotically reckless graduate student, not dental at all, and that she pegged me for that the first day of classes, when I came in late, with my bike helmet under my arm, and sat down right in front of the teacher, stuck my feet into the aisle, and burped in the silence of his pause, loud enough for three rows to hear. But it was the only seat, I was too rattled to suppress my digestive grind, and I always stuck my feet into the aisle because my legs didn't fit under the desk. It was she who wanted me, she would say, to give her life a little variety and color. When I tell her that all I've ever longed for is the opportunity to meditate over my work, she doesn't believe me.

Dana would say that she loves routine. That is how she got through a biochemistry major and through dental school, after all, with an ironclad routine that included hours of studying, but also nourishing meals, lots of sex, and irresponsible activities with me. Her vision of routine is a lot broader than most people's is. You might say that she has a genius for knowing what has to be included. She has a joke lately, though. At night, standing in the bathroom brushing her teeth, she will say, "There it goes!" or she may get up on Saturday morning and exclaim, "Zap! another one vanished!" What she is referring to is the passage of the days and weeks. A year is nothing any more. Last fall it happened that we got Lizzie the wrong snow boots, fat rather than thin, and not acceptable to Lizzie's very decided tastes. Without even a pause, Dana countered Lizzie's complaints with the promise that she could have some new ones next year, in no time at all, she seemed to be saying.

It used not to be like this. Time used to stretch and bunch up. Minutes would inflate like balloons, and the two months of our beginning acquaintance seem in retrospect as long as all the time from then until now. A day was like a cloth sack. You could always fit something else in, it would just bulge a little more. Routine is the culprit, isn't it? Something is the culprit. The other thing about routine is that it frees you for a more independent mental life, one that is partly detached from the business at hand. Even when I was pulling out all of that guy's teeth today, I wasn't paying much attention. His drama was interesting as an anecdote, but it was his. To me it was just twenty-four teeth in a row, in a row of hundreds of teeth stretching back years. I have a friend named Henry who is an oral surgeon at the University Hospital. He is still excited when he finds someone's wisdom tooth up under the eyeball, where they sometimes migrate. He can talk about his patients for hours. They come from all over the state, with facial disfigurations of all types, no two alike, Henry says. But does his enthusiasm have its source in him or in them? In ten years, is he going to move to New York City because he's tired of car wrecks and wondering about gunshot wounds? Should Dana have gone into oral surgery? I don't know any women who do that.

I sound as if we never forget that we are dentists, as if when someone smiles we automatically class their teeth as "gray range" or "yellow range." Of course we are also parents. These are my three daughters, Lizzie, Stephanie, and Leah.

They are seven, five, and two. The most important thing in the world to Lizzie and Stephanie is the social world of the grammar school playground. The most important thing to Leah is me. Apart from the fact that Lizzie and Stephanie are my daughters, I am very fond of them.

Lizzie is naturally graceful and cool, with a high, domed forehead and a good deal of disdain for things that don't suit her taste, for instance, turtleneck shirts and pajamas with feet in them. She prefers blouses and nightgowns. Propriety is important to her and wars with her extremely ready sense of humor. She knows I exploit her sense of humor to get my way, and I would like to get out of the habit of tricking her into doing things she doesn't want to do, but it is hard. The tricks always work.

Stephanie is our boy. She is tall, and strong, and not interested in rearranging the family's feelings. She would rather be out. Sometimes she seems not to recognize us in public. She feels about kindergarten the way people used to feel about going away to college: at last she is out of the house, out of her parents' control, on her own in the great world. I think she has an irrational faith that she won't always be two years younger than Lizzie.

There is a lot of chitchat in the media about how things have changed since the fifties and sixties, but I think that is because nothing has really changed at all, except the details. Lizzie and Stephanie live in a neighborbood of older houses, as I did, and walk home from the same sort of brick schoolhouse. When they get home, they watch Superman cartoons and eat Hershey bars, as I did. They swing on their swing set and play with Barbie and talk about "murdering" the boys.

They have a lot of confidence, and even power, when it

comes to the boys. To hear them tell it, the boys walk the playground in fear. Dana says, "Don't talk about the boys so much. When you grow up, you're going to resent them for it." It is tempting, from their school tales, to think of the boys as hapless dopes—always in the lowest reading group, never earning behavior stars for the week, picking their noses, exposing the elastic of their underpants. It is tempting to avoid mentioning that I was a boy once myself.

It's not as if they ever ask. The unknown age they wish to know all about is their own—what were their peculiarities as babies, and toddlers, in the misty pasts of five years ago, three years ago, last year, even. When Dana pulls out a jacket for Leah that was originally Lizzie's, Lizzie greets it with amazed delight—how can it possibly still exist, when the three-year-old who wore it has vanished without a trace?

For Leah, the misty past is still the present, and no amount of future dredging will bring to the surface her daily events of right now—her friend Tessa, at preschool, whose claim on Leah is that she wears a tiny ponytail smack on the top of her head, for example. Were we to move this year, that might furnish her with a memory of this house—a ghostly sense of lines and the fall of light that would present itself to her in some future half-waking state. I wish that Leah's state of mind weren't so unavailable to us all, including herself, because she is driving us crazy.

Dana was glad to get Leah for her third, because Leah was big and cuddly and slept through on the tenth day. There is no subsequent achievement that parent wants of child with more ardor than the accomplishment of eight hours at a stretch, during the night. Leah slept ten, and then, at three months, fourteen rock-solid nightly hours, and woke up smiling. She didn't even crawl until ten months, and could be counted on to stay happily in one place when infants who had been neonates with her were already biting electrical cords and falling down the stairs. At one, when she said her first word, it was "song," a request that Dana sing to her. Since the others were already by this time covering their ears and saying, "Oh, God!" whenever Dana launched into a tune, Dana thought that her last chance for that musical mother's fantasy was a dream come true. Everyone, especially me, liked the way Leah gave spontaneous hugs and said, "I love you," at the drop of a hat. She seemed to have an instinctive understanding of your deepest parental wishes, and a need to fulfill them. Patients who had seen her at the office would stop us and say, "That Leah is such a wonderful baby. You don't know how lucky you are." My brother would get on the phone from Cincinnati and shout in her baby ear, "Leah! Cheer up!"

Dana was overjoyed but suspicious. She would say, "No one grows up to be this nice. How are we going to wreck it?" But she would say it in a smug tone, as if experience alone assured that we wouldn't. Dana felt especially close to Leah, physically close and blindly trusting. They nursed, they sang, they read books, they got lost in the aisles of the grocery store companionably choosing this and that. "The others are like you," she often said, "but she is like me, lazy." That's what she said, but she meant "everything anyone could want." Leah was everything she could want and she, as far as she knew, was everything that Leah could want.

Not long ago, Dana got up first and went into Leah's room to get her out of her crib, and Leah said distinctly, "I want Daddy." Dana came back to the bedroom, chuckling, and I got Leah up. The next morning it happened again, but the days went on as before, with Dana sitting in the mornings and me taking the early appointments, then Dana dropping Leah at preschool, where she said, "Bye-bye, Mom, I love you."

At three I leave the office and go home to meet the schoolgirls. At five we pick up Leah, at six Dana comes home to dinner. Twelve hours of dentistry at about $100 an hour. We work alternate Saturday mornings, another $500 a week. Simple multiplication will reveal our gross income for part-time work. This is what we went to dental school for, isn't it? Since they got the dental plan over at the university, people ask me if business is better, I say, "You can't beat them off with a stick," meaning new patients. The idea of Dana and myself on the front stoop of our office building beating hordes of new patients off with sticks makes me laugh every time.

Anyway, other things were going on. They always are. A patient called me at nine thirty in the evening and said that her entire lower face was swollen and throbbing, an abscess resulting from a long overdue root canal. You remove the dead tissue and stir up the bacteria that have colonized the region and they spread. That's what an abscess is. I met her at the office and gave her six shots of novocaine, which basically numbed her from the neck up. Meanwhile, at home, Leah awakened and began crying out. Dana went in to comfort her, and Leah began crying, "I want my daddy! I want my daddy!" as if Dana were a stranger. Dana was a little taken aback, but picked Leah up, to hug and soothe her, and this made Leah so hysterical that Dana had to put her back in bed and tiptoe out, as if in shame.

By the time I had taken Mrs. Ver Steeg home and put the car in the garage, all was quiet. I was tired. I drank three beers and went to bed, and was thus unconscious for the second bout of the night, and the third. In each instance, Leah woke up crying for me, Dana went to comfort her and was sent packing. The longer she stayed and the more things she tried, the wilder Leah got. The first bout lasted from midnight to twelve thirty and the second from two forty-five until three forty. Leah began calling for me to get her out of bed at six. I woke up at last, wondering what Dana was doing, motionless beside me, and Dana said, "I won't go to her. You have to go to her." That was the beginning.

She lay on the living room carpet, rolled in her blanket, watching Woody Woodpecker cartoons from the forties. I drank coffee. She was happy. Between cartoons, she would get up and walk over to me and begin to talk. Some of the words were understandable, the names Lizzie and Stephanie, the words "oatmeal" and "lollipop." But more intelligible was the tone. She was trying to please and entertain me. She looked into my face for smiles. She gestured with her hands, shrugged, glanced away from me and back.

When Stephanie and Lizzie came down at seven, attracted by the opening theme from "Challenge of the Super-friends," she retreated to the couch. When Dana got up and staggered down the stairs in her robe, looking only for a place to deposit her exhaustion, Leah shouted, "No! Go away! Don't sit here! My couch!" She would take her oatmeal only from me. Only I was allowed to dress her. If Dana or Lizzie or Stephanie happened to glance at her, she would scowl at them and begin to cry. Dana, forgetting herself, happened to kiss her on the forehead, and she exclaimed, "Yuck! Ouch!" and wiped the kiss off. When I went to the bathroom and closed the door, she climbed the stairs behind me, saying, "I go get my daddy back." We were embarrassed. By eight forty-five, when I was ready to leave for the office, we had run out of little jokes.

It was not simply that she didn't want Dana near her, for she would allow that most of the time, it was also that she had exacting requirements for me and was indignant if I deviated from them in the slightest. If she expected to climb the stairs and find me in my bedroom and I made the mistake of meeting her in the hallway, she would burst into tears and shout, "Go back in room! Go back in room!" I would have to go back into the bedroom and pretend to be ignoring her, and wait for her to come find me and announce herself.

I don't think this ever happened to my father, who had a plumbing supply business and wore a white dress shirt to work every day. He referred to my brother and sisters and me as "the kids," in a slightly disparaging, amused tone of voice that assumed alliance with the great world of adult men, the only audience he ever really addressed himself to. I don't know anyone who calls his children "the kids." It would be like calling his spouse "the wife," not done these days. We call them "our children," "our daughters," very respectful. Would Leah thrive more certainly on a little neglect? Should we intentionally overlook her romantic obsession, as our parents might have done naturally?

At any rate, at dinner that night, there seemed no alternative to my serving her food, cutting her meat, sitting as close to her as possible. When I got up and went into the living room without taking her down from her high chair (Dana and Stephanie were still eating, Lizzie wanted me to adjust the television set), she allowed the others to leave the table without asking either of them to get her down. Dana said, "I can get you down, honey. Let me untie your strap here." Leah said, "No! No! Daddy do it."

I stayed in the living room.

Dana said, "I'll untie you and you can get yourself down. You're big enough for that."

"No! No!" said Leah. "Tie strap! Tie strap!" Dana tied it again. I stayed in the living room. Leah sat in front of her little bowl for ten minutes. Dana sent first Stephanie, then Lizzie as emissaries, first to ask if they could get her down, then if she, Dana, could get her down? Leah was adamant, with the two-year-old advantage that no one knew for sure if she knew what she was talking about, or what any of them were offering. This advantage enables her to be much more stubborn than the average speaker, whose eyes, at least, must register understanding.

After a minute or so, she began calling "Daddy! Daddy!" in a tone of voice that suggested I was far away but willing. Dana and I looked at each other. She looked hurt and resentful, then she shrugged. I got up and took Leah down from her chair. She did not greet me with the elation I expected, but after we went into the living room, she puttered around me, chattering mostly nonsense and looking to me for approval every so often. I said, "Let's go along with her for a while. It shouldn't be too hard."

Dana lifted one eyebrow and went back to her book.

It was nearly impossible. At first I thought the worst thing was the grief at parting: "Oh, Daddy! Daddy! Daddy!" hardly intelligible through the howls of betrayal. I was only going to the lumberyard or the Quiktrip, ten minutes, fifteen at the outside. Taking a child turns the errand into a forced march. "She'll be good with you," Dana would say, and she would, and the household would be relieved of screaming, but at the price of constant engagement with equipment. A snap, two threadings, and two buckles into the car seat. The reverse for getting out of the car seat. Opening an extra door for the stroller. Unfolding the stroller, locking it into stroller-rictus, wheeling it around the car, a threading and a buckle into the stroller. Up curbs, through doors, down narrow aisles, all to find a package of wood screws or a six-pack of beer. Or I could carry her, thirty-four pounds. Doing an errand by myself came to seem a lot like flying—glorious, quick, and impossible.

But grief wasn't restricted to my leaving the house. Leaving the room was enough to arouse panic, and the worst thing about it was that at first I was so unaware, and there was the labor of being trained to alert her that I was going outside or upstairs. Then there came the negotiations. One of the first things she learned to do was to tell me not to do what I had originally intended to do. After all, she had her own activities. "She loves you," said Dana. "It won't last."

There were three more elements, too. I notice that there is a certain pleasure for a meditative person like myself in laying down one thread and picking up another, as if everything isn't happening at once. One of these elements was that Dana's choir group was practicing four days a week so that they might join the chorus of the opera *Nabucco*, which was being given in our town by a very good, very urban, touring company for one night. Dana's choir director was a friend of the musical director of the company from *their* days in graduate school. The text of the chorus had to do with the Hebrews sitting themselves down by the waters of Babylon and weeping. Dana sang it every day, but in Italian. It doesn't sound as depressing in Italian as it does in English.

The second element was our summer house, which we

had purchased the fall before, in a fit of response to autumnal color. It is in the mountains not far from where we live. Since buying it, we have also bought a well, a lot of plaster, a coat of exterior housepaint, a heavy-duty lawn mower, a set of house jacks, and a wild flower book. We have identified forty-two different species of wild flowers in the area around the house alone.

The third element was that Dana fell in love with one of her fellow singers, or maybe it was the musical director. She doesn't know that I know that this was an element.

Not too long ago, the single performance of the opera *Nabucco* came and went. Leah stayed home, screaming, with the baby-sitter. Lizzie and Stephanie went along. I paid attention to the music most of the time, and the part that Dana sang about sitting down beside the waters of Babylon was very pretty, to say the least. I closed my eyes, and there were certain notes that should not have ended, that should be eternal sounds in the universe. Lizzie sat in the front seat and fell asleep on the way home. Stephanie leaned against Dana in the backseat, and also fell asleep.

In the midst of all this breathing, still dressed in her Old Testament costume and with her hair pinned up, Dana said, "I'll never be happy again." I looked at her face in the rearview mirror. She was looking out the window, and she meant it. I don't know if she even realized that she had spoken aloud. I drove into the light of the headlights, and I didn't make a sound. It seemed to me that I didn't have a sound to make.

When we got home, Leah was still awake. She was thrilled to see me, and while Dana put the others to bed and changed her clothing, I sat next to Leah's crib and held her hand while she talked to me. She talked about the moon, and her books, and her Jemima Puddleduck doll, and something else unintelligible. She perused my face for signs of pleasure. Sometimes she made gestures of ironical acceptance, shrugs of her little baby shoulders. Sometimes she sighed, as if she didn't quite understand how things work but was willing to talk about it. Are these imitations of our gestures? Or does the language itself carry this burden of mystery, so that any speaker must express it?

My eyes began to close, but Leah wasn't finished for the night, and when I slid down the wall to a reclining position, she insisted that I sit up again. It was nearly one by this time. Saturday night. I had root-canaled two, and drilled and filled two, and cleaned two more a very long time before. One of them had insisted upon talking about her sister, who had cancer of the jaw. I had been arduously sympathetic, because, of course, you must. The room was dark and filled with toys. The baby was talking. The moon shone in the window. That was the last real peace I had.

Teeth outlast everything. Death is nothing to a tooth. Hundreds of years in acidic soil just keeps a tooth clean. A fire that burns away hair and flesh and even bone leaves teeth dazzling like daisies in the ashes. Life is what destroys teeth. Undiluted apple juice in a baby bottle, sourballs, the pH balance of drinking water, tetracycline, sand in your bread if you were in the Roman army, biting seal-gut thread if you are an Eskimo woman, playing the trumpet, pulling your own teeth with a pliers. In their hearts, most dentists are certain that their patients can't be trusted with their teeth, but you can't grieve for every tooth, every mouth. You can't even grieve for the worst of them; you can only send the patient home with as many of the teeth he came in with as possible.

After a while, Leah's eyes began to take on that stare that is preliminary to sleep, and her remarks became more desultory. She continued to hold my hand. I thought about the Hebrews sitting down beside the waters of Babylon, and I began to weep, too, although as quietly as possible. I didn't see how I was going to support the total love of one woman, Leah, while simultaneously relinquishing that of another, Dana. I wasn't curious. I said my prayer, which was, "Lord, don't let her tell me about it," and shortly after that I must have fallen asleep, because the next thing I knew it was morning and I had a crick in my neck from sleeping by the window all night.

I crawled over to the half-open door and slithered through, so as not to awaken Leah. I expected to be alone, but I found Dana in her robe at the table. She was eating cold pizza. Her hair was standing up on one side, and she hadn't managed to get all the makeup off from the night before, so there were smudges around her eyes and her lips were orange. I said, "What time is it? You look terrible." She gave me a stricken look and said, "I can't believe it's over. It was so beautiful. I could sing it every night forever."

"Well, you'll sing other things." I must have sounded irritable, when I meant to sound encouraging.

"I don't want to sing other things." She sounded petulant, when she must have meant to sound tragic. I have found that there is something in the marriage bond that deflates every communication, skews it toward the ironic middle, where man and wife are at their best, good-humored and matter-of-fact. But maybe there are others who can accommodate a greater range of exhilaration and despair. Tears came into her eyes and then began running down her cheeks.

I sighed, probably sounding long-suffering, and sat down beside her and put my arms around her. Sitting down, it was awkward. I cast around for something to say. What I hit on was this: "Mrs. Hilton needs to go to a gum specialist. I scaled her yesterday for an hour, and she is exposing bone around the second and third molars."

"Have I worked on her?"

"Curly red hair, about thirty?"

"Eight-year-old X-rays of impacted wisdom teeth?"

"Won't have them out till they hurt."

"I had her. I didn't think her gums were that bad. She could go to Jerry."

"No dental insurance. Practically no money, I gather."

Dana sighed. "Lots of kids, I bet."

"Five. Sometimes she brings the eighteen-month-old and the three-year-old."

"Yeah." Now the tears really began to roll down her cheeks, and she closed her eyes tight to stop them. I had only meant to bring up a mouth, not a life. I held her tightly and repeated my prayer, and it was answered, because although she heaved a number of times, and held her breath as if about to say something, she never did.

Not long after, Lizzie and Stephanie appeared on the scene, the markers came out, the demands for paper, cereal, bananas, and milk went up, and the television went on. Lizzie and Stephanie go head to head on the drawings. Lately, Lizzie's have a lot of writing on them. Wherever the sky would ordinarily be are Lizzie's remarks, in blue, about what the figures are doing. Stephanie can't write yet, but she pays attention. Her skies are full of yellow stars. Dana went into the kitchen and sang her song about the weeping of the

Hebrews while dishing up red bowls of Cheerios and bananas. Easter was coming up, and it occurred to me that the choir might go on to something less passionate, but I couldn't imagine what it would be. They would certainly go on to fewer rehearsals every week—maybe only one.

Leah was still asleep. I remembered that I was still in my opera clothes, as formal as we get where I live, which was khaki pants, light blue shirt, sweater vest. Dana came through the dining room, and when I went up to the shower, she was already there, stepping out of her underpants with a sigh. Her breasts are wrinkled and flat from six years of nursing, but the rest of her is muscular and supple. I said, "May I join you?" Her eyes lifted to my face. It seems to me that they are very beautiful: pale, perfect blue, without a fleck of brown or green. Constant blue. Simultaneously deep-set and protuberant, with heavy, wrinkled lids. Her mother has the same eyes, only even older and therefore more beautiful. I don't know what I expected her to say. She always says yes. Now she said, "Sure." She smiled. She got out another towel. I turned on the water, got in first, and moved to the back of the tub. I reached out my hand and helped her in. We got wet, and soaped each other. She was businesslike about it, but friendly. I tried to be the same way. We talked about nitrous oxide, as I remember. We washed our hair, and she washed her face two or three times, asking each time whether the black was off her eyes.

I could not stop looking at her eyes. I wondered if the object of her affections had noticed them yet, in the sense of knowing what he was seeing rather than simply feeling the effect they had on him. She turned her back to me and bent her head under the shower, and I wondered the same thing about her back and shoulders, about the way her neck drops into her shoulders without seeming to spread, like a tulip stem.

Does he appreciate the twist of her wrist when she is picking up little things, the graceful expertise of her fingers working over that mouth, whatever mouth it is? I wondered whether the object of her affections, in fact, was the meditative sort, who separates elements, puts one thing down before picking up another, had it in him ever to have been a dentist, a mere dentist, that laughingstock of the professional community. Every time she saw me looking at her, she smiled, and every time I seemed to be doing something else, she sighed. I said, "Perk up, Dana. There's always more music."

"It's a waltz. That's what's so tragic about it. You could dance to it, but you can't." She got out, saying, "There's Leah." I rinsed off hurriedly and wiped myself down while going to Leah's room. She doesn't like to be kept waiting. She was lying on her back with her feet up on the end of the crib, calling, "Daddy! Dave! Daddy!" When she saw me, she smiled and rolled over, noting with pleasure, I suppose, the wet hair, the dripping chest, the towel, the hurry, all the signs that I had been subdued once again.

I lifted her, stripped her of wet clothes, and wiped her off with my towel. She went to the chest of drawers. I opened the bottom one for her. She chose red shorts, green slacks, and two shirts. I chose a pair of underpants and a pair of socks. She put everything on cooperatively, then admired the effect for a moment or two. I was talking the whole time: "Good morning, sweetheart! How did you sleep? What a pretty girl! Ready for breakfast? How about some Cheerios with bananas?" The usual paternal patter. I carried her downstairs, the towel wrapped around my waist, her hands upon my shoulders and her gaze upon my face. We will never know what she sees there until she finds it again, I suppose, in the face of some kid twenty years from now.

Dana was getting ready to go out. She glanced at me, and said with due formality, "I'm going to the store for milk and the newspaper. Who wants to come along?" But they were all in their nightclothes, except Leah, and so she got away without a single one of them. She looked at me and also said the right thing. "Back in a flash. Anything you want special?" I shrugged. She left. I went into the kitchen and sliced a banana with one hand, laying it on the counter and chopping at it with the paring knife, because Leah wouldn't let me put her down. Then I unscrewed the cap of the milk with one hand, poured the Cheerios with one hand, kissed Leah, and carried her to her high chair, where she consented to be put for the duration of her meal. Dana had not asked me where I spent the night, although she must have noticed that I wasn't in bed with her.

She was not back in a flash, which has to be interpreted as twenty-five minutes or a half an hour—seven minutes each way to the store, and then a generous ten for milk and newspaper. It took her an hour, and she came back much more serene than she had been since dinner the night before. She carried in her bag, said, "I got doughnuts for good girls. It's a lovely day out!" and sped into the kitchen. Oh, she was happy, happy, happy, but not exhilarated, not anything blamable or even obvious. She was simply perfectly calm, full of energy, ready for the day. No sighs. No exertion of will. I wondered if he lived nearby, but then I made myself stop wondering about him even before I might start. Leah was standing beside me, and I reached down and swung her into my arms, buried my fatal curiosity in her fleshy, baby smell.

It was a lovely day, and we decided upon a spur-of-the-minute trip to the house, to admire the plaster and the running water and to picnic on the front deck. Lizzie and Stephanie thought it was interesting that you could have a picnic at a house where there was a refrigerator and a stove, and viewed the whole plan as another example of Dana's peculiar but always instructive way of looking at things. Dana let Lizzie pack the food and Stephanie pack the toys, of which there have to be enough not only for everyone to have something to play with every moment of the trip but also to look at, consider, and disregard. It was fine with me. Dana seemed to me to be sort of like a hot-air balloon. The more weight we could hang on her, in terms of children, houses, belongings, foodstuffs, office equipment, and debts, the harder it would be for her to gain altitude.

The children sat behind us and Dana sat beside me, with her feet on the lunch basket. My strategy was to talk about patients all the way, both to remind her of what we shared and to distract her from her sadness, which sprouted as soon as we passed the city limits and grew with every mile we drove. The older children played together nicely. Lizzie, in fact, read Stephanie *Green Eggs and Ham*, and Leah was generally cordial, allowing Dana both to talk to her and to give her pieces of apple. When the apple was gone, Dana tentatively reached out her hand, as she had done often in the past, and Leah took it and held it. I drove and talked.

I have found that it is tempting to talk about every minute of the past six weeks as if the passing of every minute were an event, which was what it seemed like. I remember that car ride perfectly—the bright, early spring sunlight flooding all the windows; my own voice rising and falling in a loquacious attempt at wit, concern, entertainment, wooing; my repeated glances at her profile; the undercurrent in all my thoughts of how is she now? And now? And now? As if she were in some terminal condition.

But it was only a car ride, two hours into the country, "a dentist" with "the wife" and "the kids." It could have been 1950. I remember thinking that then, and wishing that it were—some confused thought about the fidelity of our mothers' generation, or barring the truth of that, that at least whatever it was that was present would be thirty-five years in the past, if it had taken place in 1950. Well, as I say, every minute had its own separate identity.

Some nights later, we were lying in bed after making love and I was nearly asleep. Her voice rose out of the blackness of coming somnolence like a thread of smoke. She said, "I wish we were closer." Although I was now wide awake, I maintained my breathing pattern and surreptitiously turned my chest away from her, as if in sleep, so that she couldn't hear my heart rattling in its cage. Now she would tell me, I thought, and then we would have to act. I let out a little snore, counted to twenty, and let out another one. After a minute or so, when my heart had steadied. I turned, also as if in sleep, and threw my arm over her, and hugged her tightly, as if in sleep. My nose was pressed into the back of her neck. She said, "Dave? David? Are you asleep already?" Then she sighed, and we lay there for a long time until the muscles at the back of her neck finally relaxed and she began to snore for real.

I don't know when she saw him, but I know that she did, because sometimes her sadness was cured. A long time ago, before she joined the choir, when Leah was still nursing five or six times a day, she read a book by some Middle European writer about a man who had both a wife and a mistress. I remember the way she tossed the book down and said, "You know, I always think of men who have wives and mistresses as having everything, but of women who have husbands and lovers as simply being oversubscribed." Then she laughed and went on: "I mean, where would you fit it in? Would you phone him from the grocery store with two old ladies behind you waiting to call the car service and two kids screaming in the basket?" So where did she fit it in? She was always at home when she was supposed to be. She was always in bed with me all night. She never canceled an appointment with a patient. Sometimes she was late coming home from choir practice, once a week, but she had been late in the past, and she was never more than half an hour late. But sometimes she was desperate with sadness and sometimes she was fine, and these states of mind didn't have a thing to do with me, or our household, or the office. And in addition to that, she denied that they even existed, that she was ever in turmoil or that she was ever at peace. I don't mean to say that we spoke of them. I wouldn't have allowed that under any circumstances. But she would catch me looking at her, and she would stare at me with that same stare I remembered from dental school, defiant, daring me to have any opinions about her at all.

I should say that it didn't take long for Lizzie to realize that something was up. Lizzie's situation as the oldest and her observant character make her the point man most of the time, and a lot of our battles have been fought in her digestive tract over the years. The pediatrician, whom I like a lot, does not always go for the psychosomatic explanation. In the case of Lizzie's stomach, he suggests that some children simply suffer more intense peristaltic contractions than others. Any food triggers digestion, which may or may not be painful. And it is certainly true that Lizzie has stomachaches all times of the year, all seasons of the spirit, and also tends to throw up a lot, as does Dana's sister, Frances. It has been routine on every car trip for thirty-seven years for whoever is driving Frances to pull over so that Frances can give her all on the side of the road. It is a family joke, and Frances doesn't get a lot of sympathy for it. Ditto Lizzie. Nature or nurture? My observation is that parents believe religiously in nature, while the hidden family forces that are acting to deform the plastic child are glaringly apparent to any college psych major. At any rate, Lizzie woke up every morning of the week after our trip into the country with a raging bellyache and an equal determination not to go to school, but to stay home and keep her eye on the domestic situation.

Each morning I carried her to school in tears, deposited her in the arms of Mrs. Leonard, brushed off her clutching hands, and turned on my heel to the screams of "Daddy! I need you! I need to be with you!" School, though she always settled down to her work at once, didn't make her forget my betrayal, and explanations, about how sometimes when mommies and daddies argue it makes the children feel bad, did not convince her that she wasn't actually sick. We took her temperature morning and night, promising that if it went up so much as a degree she could stay home.

I took her to the pediatrician, who put his arm around her and said that sometimes when mommies and daddies argue it makes the child feel bad. He also felt her stomach and checked her ears and throat, but she wasn't convinced. I tried to explain to him, because he is rather a friend, and certainly a fellow in the small professional community of our town, that we weren't exactly arguing, but his gaze—warm, sympathetic, resigned—flickered across my face in disbelief. Here was the child, her stomach, her panicked look, the evidence of forces at work. He said, "The stomach problem she's always had is going to be the focus of all her uneasiness. Some kids get headaches. Some get accident-prone. Every feeling is in the body as well as in the mind." His voice kept dropping lower and lower, as if he didn't know how to speak to me, a medically trained white male, and it's true, I was rather resentful. More resentful of him than of Dana or the Other. Maybe he was the Other. I wanted to punch him out.

Instead, I took Lizzie to the grocery store and let her pick out dinner. Canned corn, mashed potatoes, pork chops, orange sherbet. Not what I would have chosen, personally. Then I took her home and let her eat a Hershey bar and watch "The Pink Panther" until it was time for Stephanie to come home.

When Stephanie came home, I noticed for the first time that she had her own uneasiness. She wouldn't look at me or come in the house. She dropped her school bag without showing me any papers and went outside to play on the swings. A few minutes later she saw that one of her kindergarten friends down the street had gotten home as well, and she came and asked to go there, although this is not a friend she particularly likes, and she stayed for the rest of the afternoon, and then called to ask if she could eat dinner there. I suspect that what she would really have liked to do was move in there.

Lizzie began to cry because Stephanie didn't want to play with her, and then we had an argument about whether Stephanie loves her or not, and then I sent her to her room, and then I went up and explained to her that people have to want to play with you on their own, you can't make them, and they can't make you, either. Then I recalled examples of Lizzie not wanting to play with Stephanie, which she denied, and then I gave up, and then I went over to the preschool, leaving Lizzie by herself briefly, and picked up Leah, who, I was told, had put on her shoes and socks all by herself. She was very proud. I was, too.

Since the onset of Leah's infatuation, we had gotten into the habit of dividing the evening's tasks child by child. Dana would serve Lizzie and Stephanie and I would serve Leah. That is how it presented itself to me, although, of course, Lizzie and Stephanie had table setting and clearing to do, and were subject to discipline and the apparent dominance of the parental committee. In view of my determination not to have anything irrevocable communicated to me, this was a pretty good system, and one that I clung to. On this particular day, Dana was feeling rather blue. There was some despairing eye contact across the living room and across the kitchen. I took Leah and went out for beer, lingering over the magazine rack and talking at length with a patient I encountered about real estate taxes. I stayed away for an hour. I missed Dana terribly and wanted only to go home.

The next day at the office I missed her, too. She was right in the next room. I should say that in addition to being dentists, parents, home owners, musicians, and potential or actual adulterers, Dana and I are also employers of four people—two dental assistants and two receptionists—and office society is nearly as complex as domestic society, with the added temptation to think, unjustifiably in my experience, that it can be tinkered with and improved by a change of personnel. The receptionists are Katharyn and Dave, eight to one and one to six, six bucks an hour, and the assistants are Laura (mine) and Delilah (Dana's), eight to two and noon to six, fifteen bucks an hour. Our receptionists are always students at the university, and turn over about every two and a half years. Laura has been my assistant for five years, and Delilah came last year, replacing Genevieve. Both, as I said before, have sets of twins: Laura's fraternal, twelve years old, and Delilah's identical, four years old. Laura and Delilah also have pension plans, so, of course, we are also a financial institution, with policy decisions and long-term planning goals and investment strategies. Dave is a flirt. For convenience, he is known as "Dave," while I am known as "Dr. Dave," even, at the office, to Dana. Dana is known as "Dana." Katharyn has been engaged for three years to an Arabian engineer she met during her freshman year. Laura is divorced, edgy, bossy with the patients. Delilah is rounded, soft, an officer in the local Mothers of Twins club, which Laura has never joined. Dave flirts more with Laura than he does with Delilah, which raises the friction potential in the office about twenty-five percent. On the other hand, he is a terrific receptionist—painstaking, well organized, canny about a patient's fear of dentists. He has a sixth sense about whom to call the day before the appointment, and how to say, "We'll be expecting you, then," so that the patient doesn't dare "forget." He also does the books, so we have been able to let the bookkeeper go. He is graduating next December, a dark day.

I am so used to Laura by now that I don't know what to say about her. She has a raucous, smoke-coarsened, ironic voice, which she uses to good effect in lecturing the patients about dental hygiene. "What is this, you don't floss? You want your gums to turn to cotton candy? Believe me, if you sat in this chair and watched what comes through the door every day, you wouldn't be so optimistic. Take this. I'm going to show you." We have never talked about anything but business. Of Delilah I don't know much. She and Dana talk a lot, it seems to me, and for a long time this whispery murmur from the next office has been a kind of comforting white noise at the end of my workday. During the week, after the opera, it falls silent. Dana doesn't have much to say, or rather, what she has to say cannot be said, so she says nothing. I look blankly out the window between patients. I am sure that behind the wall Dana is doing the same thing.

What did I think I was doing on that first day of dental school? Why did I choose to pour the formless me into this particular mold? I hadn't known any dentists except the ones who worked on my own teeth. They didn't strike me as romantic figures. I was, and still am, rather struck by the mystery of teeth, of their evolution and function, of the precisely refined support system in the gums and jaws that enables a person, every person just about, simply to chew. Senseless, mindless objects, teeth, two little rows of stones in the landscape of the flesh, but as sensitive, in their way, as fingertips or lips.

I also felt the mystery of building houses back then— the way lengths of wood, hammered together with lengths of steel, created a space that people either wanted or didn't want to be inside of. I thought of architecture, but architecture was making pictures, not making buildings. Most of my fellow biology majors went to medical school or botany school or zoology school. When I considered doctoring, I used to imagine a giant body laid open on the operating table like a cadaver, but alive, and myself on a little diving board above it, about to somersault in. Not attractive. And I didn't want to spend the rest of my life fighting with some university administration about the age of my lab equipment.

This *is* what I saw myself doing: sitting here, my back hunched, the office cool and clean, the patient half asleep. I am tinkering. Making something little. But perhaps making little things belittles the self. I've noticed at conventions that dentists argue about details a lot. I wish my wife loved me. I wish her constant blue eyes would focus on me with desire instead of regret. I wonder if I haven't always been a little out of the center of her gaze, a necessary part of the life she wants to lead, but a part, only a part.

That was a Friday. The last day of a long, trying week. I suspect that Dana and I measured our time differently that week. For her, maybe, the time fell into blocks of unequal length, pivoting about the minutes she spent wherever, wherever it was that she managed to see him. My week, of course, was more orderly, and it was primarily defined by those trips with Lizzie to school each morning and lying in bed with Dana each night, wide awake and pretending to be asleep so that she wouldn't speak to me. She was, I should add, restless all week. Once, she got up at three and did something downstairs until five ten, then she came back to bed and went back to sleep. My mother used to look at us severely if we complained of not sleeping and say, "So what have you got a guilty conscience about?"

On Friday the children fell into bed at eight o'clock, practically asleep already. Dana sat knitting in front of the TV. There was an HBO showing of *Tootsie*. I went in and out, longing to sit down, unable to. Every time I went into the living room, I peered at Dana. She seemed remarkably serene, almost happy. I decided to risk it and sat down beside her on the couch. She glanced at me and smiled, pulled her yarn out of the skein with a quick, familiar snap of her wrist, and laughed at the place in the movie where Teri Garr stands up screaming. I settled into the cushions and put my arm around her shoulders. It was tempting, very tempting, not to know what I knew, but I knew that if I relaxed, she would tell me, and then I would really know it. She said, "Hard week, huh?" She sighed. I squeezed her shoulder.

"Leah doesn't make it easy, does she?"

"What if she's like this forever?"

"Remember when we used to say that about Stephanie? When she was waking up and screaming three or four times every night?"

"Do you think that was the worst?"

"It was pretty bad when Lizzie swallowed that penny."

"But that night when I had to stay in the hospital with her, I didn't dare think it was bad at all. All those babies in the otolaryngology ward were so much worse." She bit her lip, looked at the movie, turned her work, looked at me. "You know," she said, "you scare me a little. You always have. Isn't that funny?"

I thought, Compared to whom? But I said, "I don't believe you."

"It's true. You don't smile much, not the way most people do. You have this way of letting your gaze fall upon people when they attract your attention, but not smiling, nor reassuring them in any way that you aren't judging them. And you're awfully tall."

"Awfully?"

"Well, it's not awful. I mean. That's just an intensifier.

But you're a lot taller than I am. I don't think about that much, but you must be eleven inches taller than I am."

"But you've been married to me for ten years. How can you say that I scare you?"

"Remember how you used to sit me on the handlebars of your bike and coast down Cloud Street? How can I say that you don't scare me, after that?"

"Well, back then I was trying to scare you."

"Why?"

"Because you scared me. You scared everybody. You were so fucking smart."

She laughed. She turned her work. She said, "Dave, do you like me?"

I wanted to groan. I said, "I love you."

"But do you like me? If you weren't sleeping with me, would you want to talk to me and have lunch with me and stuff like that?"

"Sure."

She sighed. "But do you think that we're friends?"

"Sure."

She looked at me, and sighed again.

"Why are you sighing?" This was risky and could have led to anything, but the temptation to comfort your wife, if you love her, is a compelling one in my experience.

She thought for a moment, then looked at me and said, "I don't know. Life. Let's go to bed." She put down her knitting, turned off the light and the television, and led me by the hand up the stairs. She took off my shirt and my pants. Reached up to my awfully tall shoulders and ran her fingers across them. I undid the tie of her robe and cupped her breasts in my hands. She ran her hands down my chest, exploring, trying me out, looking at me again, over her shoulder in a way. I'm not going to say that I could even begin to resist.

I am thirty-five years old, and it seems to me that I have arrived at the age of grief. Others arrive there sooner. Almost no one arrives much later. I don't think it is years themselves, or the disintegration of the body. Most of our bodies are better taken care of and better-looking than ever. What it is, is what we know, now that in spite of ourselves we have stopped to think about it. It is not only that we know that love ends, children are stolen, parents die feeling that their lives have been meaningless. It is not only that, by this time, a lot of acquaintances and friends have died and all the others are getting ready to sooner or later. It is more that the barriers between the circumstances of oneself and of the rest of the world have broken down, after all— after all that schooling, all that care. Lord, if it be thy will, let this cup pass from me. But when you are thirty-three, or thirty-five, the cup must come around, cannot pass from you, and it is the same cup of pain that every mortal drinks from. Dana cried over Mrs. Hilton. My eyes filled during the nightly news. Obviously we were grieving for ourselves, but we were also thinking that if *they* were feeling what *we* were feeling, how could they stand it? We were grieving for them, too. I understand that later you come to an age of hope, or at least resignation. I suspect it takes a long time to get there.

On Saturday, Dana asked me to take the children up to the house in the country and maybe spend the night. The beds, she said, were made. There was plenty of firewood. We would, she said, have a good time. She would join us for dinner, after the Saturday-morning office hours. It was very neatly done. I said, "Maybe that's a good idea. But you could take them and let me do the morning work." Her face fell into her shoes. I said, "No, I would like to go into the country, I think."

It was another sunny day, but cold. Each child was bundled against the weather, her coat vigorously zipped, her hat pulled down over her ears with a snap, her mittens put on and tucked into her sleeves. To each one, Dana said, "Now you be nice to Daddy, and don't make him mad, okay? I'll finish my work and come for dinner, so I will see you very soon. Tonight we'll have a fire in the wood stove and make popcorn and have a good time, okay?" And each child nodded, and was hugged, and then strapped in. Leah sat in front, eyeing me with pleasure. We drove off.

I couldn't resist looking at Lizzie and Stephanie again and again in the rearview mirror. They were astonishingly graceful and attractive, the way they leaned toward each other and away, the way their heads bent down and then popped up, the way their gazes caught, the way they ignored each other completely and stared out the windows. The pearly glow of their skin, the curve of their cheeks and foreheads, the expressiveness of their shoulders. I felt as if I had never seen them before.

After about an hour, Lizzie began feeling anxious. She asked for milk, said she was hot, subsided. Stephanie sat forward and said, "Is the pond still frozen, do you think? Can we slide on the pond?"

"I don't know. We'll see."

"Daddy, my stomach feels funny." This was Lizzie.

"You shouldn't have drunk so much milk."

"I didn't. I took three swallows." Then she panicked. "I'm going to throw up! Stop! I'm going to throw up!"

"Oh, God," said Stephanie.

"Oh, God," said Leah, mimicking her perfectly. I pulled over. Lizzie was not going to throw up, but I got out of the car, opened her door, took her to the side of the road, bent over her, holding her forehead in one hand and her hair in the other. All the formalities. Her face turned red and she panted, but though we stood there for ten minutes, she neither gagged nor puked. I felt her body stiffen, and we straightened up. There were tears in her eyes, and she said petulantly, "I was going to."

"I know. It's okay."

But it wasn't okay with Stephanie. As soon as I pulled onto the highway again, she said, "I don't see why we always have to stop. She never does anything."

"I was going to."

"You were not."

"How do you know? I was."

"Were not."

"Stephanie—" This was me. I looked in the rearview mirror. Stephanie's tongue went out. Leah said, admiringly, "Stephanie—" The argument subsided, to be resumed later. They always are.

Now Lizzie said, "Why are we going to the house? I don't want to go. We went there last week."

"Me, neither," said Stephanie. "I was going to play My Little Ponies with Megan." She must have just remembered this, because it came out with a wail.

"It'll be fun," I said, but I wasn't as convincing as Dana, who must have cast a spell to get us to leave, because I didn't want to go to the country, either. I glanced at my watch. It was ten o'clock. We could have turned around and been home before lunch, but we didn't. There was no place for us there.

At the next K-mart, I turned into the parking lot with a flourish and took them straight to the toy department.

After the dinner that Dana missed and the bedtime she failed to arrive for, I turned out all the lights and sat on the porch in the dark, afraid. I was afraid that she was dead. I wished she had a little note on her that said, "My family is at the following telephone number." But, then, a note could be burned up in the wreck, as could her purse, the registration to the car, all identifying numbers on the car itself. Everything but her teeth. I imagined myself telling the children that she had gone off with another man, then some blue-garbed policeman appearing at the office this week or next with Dana's jaw. I would recognize the three delicate gold inlays I had put there, the fixed prosthesis Marty Crockett did in graduate school, when her tooth broke on a sourball. I would take her charred mandible in my hand and weigh it slightly. Would I be sadder than I was now?

Headlights flared across the porch and she drove up with a resolute crunch of gravel. The car door opened. She seemed to leap out and fly up the steps, throw open the door to the dark house, and vanish. She didn't see me, and I didn't say a word. I saw her, though. I saw the look on her face as if my eyeballs were spotlights. She was a soul desperate to divulge information. I got up quietly and walked down the steps, avoiding the gravel, and tiptoed across the front meadow to the road.

So how does the certainty that your wife loves another man feel? Every feeling is in the body as well as in the mind, that's what he said. But the nerves, for the most part, end at the surface, where they flutter in the breezes of worldly stimulation. Inside, they are more like freeways—limited access, running only from major center to major center. I have to admit that I don't remember much Gross Anatomy, so I don't know why it feels the way it feels, as if all your flesh were squeezing together, squeezing the air out of your lungs, squeezing the alveoli so they can never inflate again. More than that, it is as if soon there might be no spaces left inside at all, no conduits for fluids, even. Only the weight of solid flesh, the conscious act of picking up this heavy foot, and then this heavy foot, reaching this cumbersome hand so slowly that the will to grasp is lost before the object is touched. But when the light went on and the door opened and Dana peered into the darkness, I jumped behind a tree as sprightly as a cricket. Every feeling is in the mind as well as in the body. She went back into the house. The light on the stairs went on, then in the upstairs hall, then in the bathroom. A glow from the hall shone in each of the two children's rooms, as she opened their doors to check on them, then the window of our room lit up. It seemed to me that if I could stay outside forever she would never tell me that she was going to leave me, but that if I joined them inside the light and the warmth, the light and warmth themselves would explode and disappear.

I went around the side of the house, placed myself in the shadow of another tree, and watched the window to our bedroom. The shade was drawn, and I willed Dana to come and put it up, to open the window and show me her face without seeing me. She has a thin face, with high, prominent cheekbones and full lips. She has a way of smiling in merriment and dropping her eyelids before opening her eyes and laughing. In dental school I found this instant of secret, savored pleasure utterly beguiling. The knowledge that she was about to laugh would provoke my own laughter every time. I wonder if the patients swim up out of the haze of nitrous oxide and think that she is pretty, or that she is getting older, or that she looks severe. I don't know. I haven't had a cavity myself in fifteen years. Laura cleans my teeth twice a year and that's it for me. The shade went up, the window opened, and Dana leaned out and took some deep breaths. She put her left hand to her forehead and said, in a low, penetrating tone, "Jesus." She sighed deep, shuddering sighs, and wrapped her robe tightly around her shoulders. "Jesus," she said. "Oh, Jesus. Jesus Christ. Oh, my God." I had never heard her express herself with so little irony in my whole life. A cry came from the back of the house, and she pushed herself away from the window, closing it. Moments later, the glow from the hall light shone in Leah's room.

Now I went back to where I had been standing before. The windows in the children's rooms faced north and west, and hadn't received their treatments yet, so everything Dana did was apparent in an indistinct way. She went to the crib and bent over it. She stood up and bent over it again. She held out her arms, but Leah did not come into them. I could hear the muffled staccato of her screams. Dana stood up and put her hands on her hips, perplexed and, probably, annoyed. There was a long moment of this screaming; then Dana came to one of the windows and opened it. She leaned out and said, "David Hurst, goddamn you, I know you're out there!" She didn't see me. She turned away, but left the window open, so I could hear Leah shouting, "No! No! Daddy! Daddy!" Now the glow of the hall light appeared in the windows of Lizzie and Stephanie's room, and then Lizzie appeared next to Dana. Dana bent down and hugged her, reassuringly, but the screaming didn't stop. At last, Dana picked Leah up, only with a struggle, though, and set her down on the floor. I didn't move. I was shivering with the cold, and it took all my will not to move. It was like those nights when Stephanie used to wake up and cry. Each of us would go in and tuck her in and reassure her, then go out resolutely and shut the door. After that we would lie together in bed listening to the cries, sometimes for hours. Every fiber in your body wants to pick that child up, but every cell in your brain knows that if you pick her up tonight, she will wake up again tomorrow night and want to be picked up. Once, she cried from midnight until about seven in the morning. The pediatrician, I might add, said that this was impossible. You could say that it is impossible for a man to pull all of his own teeth with only the help of a few swallows of whiskey. Nothing is impossible. I know a man who dropped his baby in her GM Loveseat down a flight of stairs. Having carried that burden uncountable times myself, having wrapped my arms and my fingers tightly around that heavy, bulky object, I might have said that it was impossible for a father to drop his child, but it happened. Nothing is impossible. And so I didn't move.

Stephanie got up and turned on the light in her room. Dana turned on the light in Leah's room. Soon there were lights all over the house. After that, the light of the television, wanly receiving its single channel. I saw them from time to time in the downstairs windows, Dana passing back and forth, pausing once to clench her fists and shout. What she was shouting was, "So shut up, just shut up for a moment, all right?" A sign that she has had it. They always shut up. Then she opens her fists and spreads her fingers and closes her eyes for a moment and takes a deep breath and says, "Okay. Okay." She went out of view. The light went on in the kitchen, and she reappeared, carrying glasses of milk.

She went away again. She reappeared carrying blankets and sleeping bags. Then they all must have lain down or sat down on the floor, because all I saw after that was the wall of the living room, with half a Hundertwasser print and the blue of the television flickering across it. I looked at my watch. It was a quarter to two.

At two thirty, lights began going out again, first in the kitchen, then the dining room. The television went off. Dana passed the window, carrying a wrapped-up child, Leah, because that was the room she went into. She went to the window and closed it. Then she carried up Lizzie and Stephanie, one at a time. Don't stumble on those blankets going up the stairs, I thought. The living room light went out. The hall light. The bathroom light. The light in our room. It was three by now. The house was dark. I imagined sleep rising off them like smoke, filtering through the roof and ascending to the starry sky. I stayed outside. The sun came up about six. I went inside and made myself a big breakfast. I sat over it, reading the paper from the day before, until nearly eight thirty, when Dana came down. She was furious with me and didn't speak. I estimated that her pride might carry us through another three or even four days without anything being communicated.

I got up and walked out, leaving all the dirty dishes. Was I furious with her? Was that why I had taken this revenge? In the interests of self-knowledge, I entertained this possibility. Ultimately, however, I didn't care what my motives were. The main thing was that I had invested a new and much larger sum in my refusal to listen to any communications from my wife, and I saw that I would have to protect my investment rather cannily from now on.

For someone who has been married so long, I remember

what it was like to be single quite well. It was like riding a little moped down a country road, hitting every bump, laboring up every hill. Marriage is like a semi, or at least a big pickup truck jacked up on fat tires. It barrels over everything in its path, zooming with all the purpose of great weight and importance into the future. When I was single, it seemed to me that I made up my future every time I registered for classes. After I paid my fees, I looked down at that little $4,000 card in my hand and felt the glow of relief. It was not that I was closer to being a dentist. That was something I couldn't imagine. It was that four more months of the future were visible, if only just. At the end of every term, the future dropped away, leaving me gasping.

Dana, however, always had plans. She would talk about them in bed after we had made love. She talked so concretely about each one, whether it was giving up dentistry and going to Mazatlán, or whether it was having Belgian waffles for breakfast if only we could get up two hours hence, at five thirty, in time to make it to the pancake house before our early classes, that it seemed to me that all I had to do was live and breathe. The future was a scene I only had to walk into. What a relief. And that is what it has been like for thirteen years now. I had almost forgotten that old vertigo. I think I must have thought I had grown out of it.

The day after I stayed up all night, which I spent working around the country house, clearing up dead tree limbs and other trash, pruning back this and that, the future dropped away entirely, and I could not even have said whether I would be at my stool, picking up my tools, the next morning. The very biological inertia that propelled me around the property, and from meal to meal, was amazing to me. I was terrified. I was like a man who keeps totting up the days that the sun has risen and making odds on whether it will rise again, who can imagine only too well the deepening cold of a sunless day. I gather that I was rather forbidding, to boot, because everyone stayed away from me except Leah, who clambered after me, dragging sticks and picking up leaves, and keeping up a stream of talk in her most man-pleasing tones.

Dana supported her spirits, and theirs, with a heroic and visible effort. They drove to one of the bigger supermarkets, about twenty miles away, and brought everything back from the deli that anyone could possibly have wanted—bagels, cream cheese mixed with lox, cream cheese mixed with walnuts and raisins, French doughnuts, croissants with chocolate in them, swordfish steaks for later, to be grilled with basil, heads of Buttercrunch lettuce, raspberry vinegar and olive oil, bottles of seltzer for Lizzie's stomach, *The New York Times*, the Chicago *Tribune*, for the funny papers. She must have thought she could lose herself in service, because she was up and down all day, getting one child this and another child that, dressing them so that they could go out for five minutes, complain of the cold, and be undressed again. She read them about six books and fiddled constantly with the TV reception. She sat on the couch and lured them into piling on top of her, as if the warmth of human flesh could help her. She was always smiling at them, and there was the panting of effort about everything she did. I wondered what he had done to her, to give her this desperation. Even so, I stayed out of the way. Any word would be like a spark in a dynamite factory. I kept Leah out of her hair. That is what I did for her, that is the service I lost myself in.

At dinner, when we sat across from each other at the old wooden table, she did not lift her eyes to my face. The portions she served me were generous, and they rather shamed me, as they reminded me of my size and my lifelong greed for food. I complained about the fish. It was a little undercooked. Well, it *was* a little undercooked, but I didn't have to say it. That was the one time she looked at me, and it was a look of concentrated annoyance, to which I responded with an aggressive stare. About eight we drove back to town. I remember that drive perfectly, too. Leah was sleeping in her car seat beside me, Lizzie was in the back, and Dana had Stephanie in her car. At stoplights, my glances in the rearview mirror gave me a view of her unyielding head. At one point, when I looked at her too long and missed the turning of the light, she beeped her horn. Lizzie said that her stomach hurt. I said, "You can stand it until we get home," and Lizzie fell silent at once, hearing the hardness in my voice. It was one of those drives that you remember from your own childhood and swear you will never have, so frightening, that feeling of everything wrong but nothing visibly different, of no future. But of course, there is a future, plenty of future for the results of this drive to reveal themselves, like a long virus that visits the child as a simple case of chicken pox and returns over and over to the adult as a painful case of shingles.

I should say that what I do remember about Dana, from the beginning, is a long stream of talk. I don't, as a rule, like to talk. That is why I preferred those rubber dams. That is why I like Laura. Dana is right, people who don't talk and rarely smile seem threatening. I am like my mother in this, not my father, whose hardware store was a place where a lot of men talked. They wandered among the bins of traps and U joints and washers and caulk, and they talked with warmth and enthusiasm, but also with cool expertise, about the projects they were working on. My father walked with them, drawing them out about the details, then giving advice about products. When my father was sick or out of town, my mother worked behind the counter and receipts plummeted. "I don't know"—that's what she answered to every question. And she didn't. She didn't know what there was or where it might be or how you might do something. It was not that she didn't want to know, but you would think it was from the way she said it: "Sorry, I don't know." Snap. Her eyelids dropped and her lips came together. I suspect that "I don't know" is the main sentiment of most people who don't talk. Maybe "I don't know, please tell me." That was my main sentiment for most of my boyhood. And Dana did. She told me everything she was thinking, and bit by bit I learned to add something here and there. I didn't know, for example, until the other night that I don't smile as much as most people. She told me. Now I know.

What is there to say about her voice? It is hollow. There is a vibration in it, as of two notes, one slightly higher than the other, sounding at the same time. This makes her singing voice very melodious, but the choir director doesn't often let her sing solo. He gives someone with purer tones the solo part, and has Dana harmonize. These small groups of two or three are often complimented after the choir concerts. It is in this hollow in her voice that I imagine the flow of that thirteen-year stream of talk. She is a talker. I suppose she is talking now to him, since I won't let her talk to me.

Monday night, after a long, silent day in the office to the accompaniment of extra care by the office staff that made me very uncomfortable, we went to bed in silence. She woke up cursing. "Oh," she said, "oh shit. Ouch." I could feel her reaching for her feet. When we were first married, she used to get cramps in her insteps from pointing her toes in her sleep. Some say this is a vitamin deficiency. I don't know.

Anyway, I slithered under the covers and grabbed her feet. What you do is bend the toes and ankles back, and then massage the instep until the knot goes away. Massage by itself doesn't work at all; you have to hold on to the toes so that they don't point by mistake, for about five minutes. I did. She let me. While I was holding on to her feet I felt such a welling up of desire and pain and grief that I began to heave with dry sobs. "Dave," she said. "Dave." Her hollow voice was regretful and full of sorrow. In the hot dark under the covers, I ran my thumbs over her insteps and pushed back her toes with my fingers. Your wife's feet are not something, as a rule, that you are tactilely familiar with, and I hadn't had much to do with her feet for eight or nine years, so maybe I was subject to some sort of sensual memory, but it seemed to me that I was twenty-five years old and ragingly greedy for this darling person whom I had had the luck to fool into marrying me. Except that I wasn't, and I knew I wasn't, and that ten minutes encompassed ten years, and I was about to be lost. When the cramps were out of her feet, I knelt up and threw off the covers, and said, "Oh, God! Dana, I'm sorry I'm me!" That's what I said. It just came out. She grabbed me by the shoulders and pulled me down on top of her and hugged me tightly, and said in a much evener voice, "I'm not sorry you're you."

And so, how could she tell me then? She couldn't, and didn't. I think she was sorry I was me, sorry that I wasn't him in bed with her. But when husbands express grief and fear, wives automatically comfort them, and they are automatically comforted. Years ago, such an exchange of sorrow would have sent us into a frenzy of lovemaking. It did not this time. She held me and kissed my forehead, and I was comforted but not reassured. We went back to sleep and got up at seven to greet the daily round that is family life. Zap, she used to say, there goes another one.

I was worried about her and she was worried about me, and that was an impasse that served my purposes for most of that week. God knows what the bastard was doing to her, but she was very reserved, careful, good, and sad. She went to the grocery store a lot. Maybe she was calling him from there, standing in the phone booth with two children in the basket and a line of old ladies behind her waiting to call the car service.

Each of my children favors one sense over the other. Lizzie has been all eyes since birth. We have pictures of her at nine days old, her eyes focused and glittering, snapping up every visual stimulation. She is terrific at finding things and has been since she could talk. It took us a while to believe her, but now we believe her every time. She doesn't stare, either. She glances. She stands back and takes in wholes. It seems to me that her eyes are the source of her persnickety taste and her fears. She simply cannot bear certain color combinations, for example. They offend her physically. Likewise, what she sees is far away from her, out of her control, and so makes her afraid. She rushes in, gets closer, so that she can look more carefully. But it is hard for her to reach out and touch or rearrange. Fear intervenes. She only looks, she feels no power.

Stephanie is the wild beast who is soothed by music. She has always heard things first, looked for them second. She often looks away from what she is paying attention to, making her seem evasive, but really she is listening. She is the only child I've ever known who doesn't interrupt. I don't even know if she listens to words as much as to tones, to the rhythms of sentences and the pitch of voices. Will she be a musician? She likes music. But she likes the sound of traffic, too, and the sound of cats in the backyard, and the cries of birds and the rustle of leaves. She simply likes the way the world sounds, and she listens to it. She comes closer than Lizzie does, but she doesn't seem to respond to what goes in at all, except with a single, final look, to make sure, maybe, that what is heard has a source. Then she backs away. Is she the one I should worry about?

Leah sat up at five months and reached for the toys that were in front of her. It took her another five months to crawl. Yes, she was big and fat, but more than that, she was satisfied. Her hands were huge, and she could hold two blocks in each of them when she was six months old. Hand to mouth. You couldn't keep anything out of her mouth. Now it seems as though she doesn't recognize anything without touching it. She runs her hands over my face. She holds on tight. She snuggles. Standing in front of a table of toys, she is as satisfied as a human can be, and she has stretches of concentration that Lizzie and Stephanie don't begin to match, although they are five and three years older than she is. If you distract her, she looks drugged for a moment. Drugged by touch.

And so I have three separate regrets. What does Lizzie see? What does Stephanie hear? What unsatisfied, yearning tension does Leah feel in my flesh when she snuggles against me and puts her hands on my shoulders? There is no hiding from them, is there? And there is no talking to them. They don't understand what they understand. I am afraid. I should call the pediatrician, but I don't. I think, as people do, that everything will be all right. But even so, I can't stop being afraid. They are so beautiful, my daughters, so fragile and attentive to family life.

I wish they were boys and completely oblivious, as I

was. I could not have said, before I met Dana, whether my parents' marriage was happy or not. I didn't know. She told me. She said, "Your parents are so dissimilar, aren't they? I mean, your father is sociable and trusting and all business, and your mother just doesn't know what to make of things, does she? They are a truly weird combination." We were twenty-two. She had spent her first half hour with them, and this was what she came out with, and that is what I have known about them ever since.

The next day a new patient came in, a heavyset, pugnacious man about my age. I poked around in his mouth and said, "Besides your present cavities, you have some very poorly filled teeth here." He sat up and looked at me and said, "You know, I've never been to a dentist who thought much of what was done to your teeth before him. And I'll say this, you'd better be cheap, because five years from now, some guy's going to tell me he's got to redo all your work, too." He sat back and looked out the window for a second, but he must have thought that the ice was broken, because he started right in again. "Doctors never say boo about what they see. I mean, some guy could cut off your healthy leg and leave the bad one, and you wouldn't get another doctor to admit the guy had made a mistake."

"Hmm," I said.

"I don't know," he said. "Things are more fucked every day."

"Open, please," I said.

"I mean, I don't know why I'm sitting here having my teeth fixed. It's going to cost me a lot of money that I could spend having the other stuff fixed. By the way, don't touch the front teeth. I play the trumpet, and if you touch the front teeth, then I'll have to change my embouchure."

I said, "Open, please."

"Well, I'm not sure I want to open. I mean, if you don't do anything, then I can spend my money on therapy or something that might really improve my life."

"We do ask patients to pay for appointments they don't keep. If you're uneasy about the discomfort, we have a lot of ways to make sure—"

"Hell, I don't care if it pinches, like you guys all say. I don't care if it hurts like shit. I just want to feel I'm not wasting my time."

"Proper dental care is never a—"

"My wife made this appointment for me. Now I've lost my job, and she's kicked me out. But she sent me this little card, telling me to go here, and I came. I mean, I can't—"

"Mr. Slater, please open your mouth so that we can get on with it."

"I can't believe she kicked me out, but I really can't believe she cares whether or not I go to the dentist."

"I don't know, Mr. Slater. But you are wasting my time and yours, too."

"Didn't you say you'd get paid, anyway?"

"That's our policy, yes."

"How long does it take you to fill a couple of teeth?"

"About half an hour."

"Then just let me talk. I'll pay you."

"I don't like to talk, Mr. Slater," I said. "I'd rather fill teeth."

"But I'll pay you the money I should be paying a psychiatrist."

I put down my mirror and my probe. Dana passed the door and glanced in, curious. Her eyes left an afterimage of blue. Slater said, "That your wife?"

"What do you want to talk about, Mr. Slater?"

He sat back and deflated with a big sigh. He looked out the window. I did, too. Finally, he said, "Hey, I don't know. Go ahead and fill a couple of teeth. You're probably better at that, anyway."

"That's what I'm trained to do, Mr. Slater."

He made no reply, and I filled two molars, right lower. He didn't speak again, but every time I changed my position or asked him to do something, he fetched up a bone-quivering sigh. His front teeth, I should say, were a mess. A brittle net, crooked, destined for loss. He left without speaking to me again, and paid with his MasterCard.

After he left I wanted him back. I wanted the navy-blue collarless jacket that he wouldn't take off. I wanted the Sansabelt slacks that stretched tight over his derriere. I wanted the loafers. I wanted him to tell me about his wife. He didn't smile much. He had a rough way of speaking. He was tall and not a pleasant man. It seemed to me that I could have drilled his teeth without novocaine, man to man, and it would have relieved us both.

He was with me all the rest of the afternoon. I imagined him leaving the office when I did. I imagined how he would walk, how he would get in his car, how he would drive down the street—thrusting and pugnacious, jamming the pedals, hand close to the horn all the time. Grief, I saw, had loosened him up, as if at the joints, and up and down his vertebrae. He had become a man who would do or say anything, would toss back his head or fling out his arms in a gesture impossible before. He wouldn't leave me alone. I felt bitterly sorry for him all afternoon. It seemed to me that his fate would be an ill one, and mine, too. All of our fates.

By the time Dana came home, I couldn't stop doing

things as Slater might have done them. I was talkative and aggressive. I put my hands on her shoulders and turned her around so that she would look at me. I wandered around the kitchen, opening cupboards and slamming them shut. I talked about all of my patients except Slater at boring length. My voice got loud. Dana shrank and shrank. At first she laughed; then, with a few sidelong glances in my direction, she began to scuttle. I wondered if Slater's wife was just then doing exactly the same thing. But she wasn't. She had kicked him out, and I could certainly see why. Finally I stopped. I just stopped where I was standing, with my mouth gaping open, and Dana and I traded a long glance. I said, "What time is dinner?"

"About half an hour. Dave—"

"I'm going out. I'll be back, okay?" Slater wouldn't have asked in that way for permission. Neither would Dave Hurst, a month ago. I slammed out the back door and got into the car.

After I left Dana, Slater left me, and Dana joined me. I had hardly seen her back at the house, the whole time I was hovering around her, but now I could practically smell her, feel the vigor of her presence. As a rule, I don't know what she looks like. I don't think I have known, since the beginning, before everything about her looks became familiar to me, and saturated with feeling. As I drove along in the car, a picture of what she looks like came to me for the first time in years. And I thought, She is pretty, but she is getting a little prim-looking, with her gold button earrings and the gold chains around her neck. She wears neat blouses in the office, even now, in the midst of passion. And as this picture came to me, it also came to me that this passion was unbearable to her, and that the only way she knew to make it bearable was to pour herself into it as well as everything else, the way she has always done. I stepped on the gas, and soon I was streaming down the interstate at 92 miles per hour. "Lord," I said, "let me fly. Give me that miracle to ease this pain." I pushed the car up to 100. I hadn't had a car into three figures in seventeen years, since Kevin Mills let me gas his father's Oldsmobile 98 up to 115 the summer after we graduated from high school. I went fast, but I didn't fly. Instead, I thought of my children and turned back at the next exit. I realized that the object of Dana's affections had refused her.

At the dinner table, Slater invaded me again. I was cutting Leah's meat and she was complaining that the pieces were too large, so I cut them and cut them until they were nearly mush. Then she said, "I don't like it." I sat back and looked at her, then around the table at the others, and it seemed to me that I was Slater, visiting for dinner. The woman was blond, sort of pretty and nice enough, I thought, but her children were horrible, the oldest sullen and suspicious—clank, clank-clank went her knife and fork on the plate—the next one an oblivious blonde, masticating her food with annoying languor, and the third irritable and squawking. At last, inevitably, Leah smacked her bowl and it landed upside down on the floor. As Slater, I waited for their mother to do something about it. As my wife, Dana looked at me expectantly. Leah looked at me expectantly. I pretended to be their father. I jumped up and grabbed Leah out of her chair, and said in gruffish tones, "That's enough. I'm putting you into your bed." And I carried her upstairs. The windows were dirty and the sills needed vacuuming, and there were toys all over the floor of the child's room. The responsibility for all this seemed put upon me, and I stomped down the stairs, shouting, "Be quiet! Stop yelling! You can come down in five minutes."

"Dave," said Dana.

I answered to this name.

"I don't think you should shout at her like that."

"Somebody has to. Maybe nobody has enough. You don't. What the fuck is going on around here?"

Dana looked up fearfully. "Nothing. Nothing is going on, just everything the same. Why don't you sit down and—"

Now I really was Slater. "Everything's more fucked every day."

Lizzie and Stephanie had put down their forks and were staring out at me from under their foreheads, as if they couldn't take the full blast of me in their faces, but couldn't resist a look.

Dana said, "Why are you like this? Why are you so angry all the time? It's unbearable."

"I'm not angry all the time! I'm not really angry now."

"Listen to yourself! Can't you hear what you're saying?"

"But it's true, things are more fucked every day! Every day! Every day is worse!"

"No, it isn't! It isn't. Don't say that. I won't listen to that! You've always said that! I hate it."

"I have not always said that. I just realized it today."

"You have." She burst into tears. I was bitterly hurt and angry. Her greatest lifelong sin seemed to me to be that she didn't agree with me about the way the world is. I thought, I could accept anything else, let her love him, let her fuck him, let her talk to him forever, but give me this little agreement that I've never had before. I said, or rather shouted, "Admit that I'm right. Admit that every day is worse!"

"I won't!"

I could kill you, I thought.

"What did you say?"

"I didn't say anything."

"You said you could kill me." I looked into each horrified face and saw that I had said it, or Slater had said it. I groaned. "I didn't mean to say it."

"But you thought it."

"I can't control my thoughts."

"You thought you could kill me."

"I don't know what I thought. I thought a lot of things. I think all the time." I sat down and looked first at Lizzie and then at Stephanie, and I said, "A person can think anything that they want, because there is no way to make yourself not think things. But you don't want to do everything you think. I'm sorry. I think I'll go out for a little while." And then Slater and I slammed out of the house and got in the car again, although my father always used to say, in every crisis, "At least don't get in the car." And he never did.

Slater kept wanting to stop at a bar. Or at a gas station to pick up a couple of six-packs. Dave didn't think this was an especially good idea, but he did think he deserved something. What Dave really thought was that a responsible professional man, owner of two homes, employer of four persons, parent of three daughters, and lifelong meditative personality ought to be able to control himself. He also thought that his wife, a responsible professional woman, and ditto ditto ditto, if not ditto, ought to have been able to control herself, too. We stopped, Slater and I, at a rest area about thirty miles up the interstate, and there, without the benefit of a six-pack, we stood back from the road in the gloom of a chilly night and we screamed and screamed and screamed. After screaming, while noticing that we had screamed our throat into raw throbbing, we noticed the stars. They lay across the dark blue sky like sugar and diamonds sprinkled together. And Lord, how they shamed the flesh.

In the exhausted backwash of all this verbalizing, I realized that my plan not to be communicated with was at greater risk than ever, because I had made myself so unpleasant that it was likely she would flee to him, or at least flee from me at whatever cost. In fact, my success now rested with his resolution not to have her. Only with that. I wondered what it was about her, her circumstances or her person, that gave him pause. Or maybe it was her intrinsic passion. Maybe he had thought he saw in her cool blondness some sort of astringent distance, and now he saw that between Dana and a desired object there was no distance allowed at all. Maybe he was dazzled by the neat blouses and the deft workmanship into not seeing the defiant, greedy stare. Maybe he saw only the established dentist, not the determined dental student, the stainless-steel blonde in the doorway of the classroom, radiating tensile strength like heat. Appearances aren't deceiving, I think, but you have to know where to look.

I should say that it was hard for me not to see her as a dramatic figure. I always had seen her that way. Maybe, in fact, he only viewed her as something of a bore, a little thing, a mere woman passing through his life. I don't know. I never even saw him. I got home about twelve and sneaked into bed. Dana was already asleep. There is something I have noticed about desire, that it opens the eyes and strikes them blind at the same time. These days, when I lie awake at night and think about those early spring weeks, the objects of the world as they were then appear to me with utter clarity. Edges sharp, colors bright, movements etched into the silvery mirror of light and air. When I used to think of the word "confusion," I would think of a kind of gray mist, but that is not what confusion is. Confusion is perfect sight and perfect mystery at the same time. Confusion is seeing without knowing, as if the optic nerves were still attached but the hemispheres of the brain were parted. Desire is confusion vibrating in the tissues.

Confusion and desire also include the inability to keep quiet. One of the things I remember with embarrassing clarity is all the talking I did, all the statements I made about every possible thing. They were all assertions, bombast, a waste of breath. Could I have shut up? The world was beautiful during those weeks—chill, sunny, gold-green, severe undecorated shapes of mountains, tree limbs, stones, clouds, floating together and together in a stream of configurations as the eye rolled past them. If I had it again, I would look at it better.

About this time we had what Dana would call "an early warning." News of the impending disaster came first to Laura, through her cousin in California, then to Dave from his mother two states away. Vomiting, high temperatures in both children and adults, lethargy, sore throat, possible ear complications. Dana told Dave to rearrange our schedules for about a week, so that the illness could pass through the body of the family with as little disruption as possible. It isn't unusual—the note from the school nurse reporting a case of chicken pox, the patient confiding, just before he opens his jaws, that he is feeling a little woozy, and then he leans back and out it comes, the miasma of contagion. Once each winter, if we are lucky, twice if we are not, the great family reunion that is the flu, or strep throat. The family patients have their characteristic styles of illness, and Lizzie is truly the worst, since she can't stand discomfort but fights the medicine. Dana is hardly any better and seems to get a certain amount of relief from simply cursing, which doesn't give the rest of us any relief at all. And me? Dana says that I am the one who haunts the house with a martyred air. I ask for a glass of orange juice, she says, and then, before she has a chance to get it, I turn up beside the refrigerator, wounded to the quick by her failure of care, and pour it myself. Yes, yes, yes. I wasn't eager, given our circumstances, to take on this flu.

The patients, now transformed into vectors, came without cease. I leaned over them. I picked up one instrument at a time and set each down. I wanted to be careful and not angry. I wanted, in fact, not to be myself, but I didn't want to be Slater, either. None of the patients really replaced him in the chair, though, and when Dana passed the door, or spoke in the outer office, his ears pricked with that sleazy curiosity of his. "That your wife?" he kept saying. My private revenge against him was that I knew that his front teeth were going to disintegrate, and that his embouchure wouldn't be his for long, no matter what. Slater was an insensitive fellow, though, and didn't care what I knew. He also wanted to sit sullenly in the office and eat steak subs with cheese and drink coffee every day for lunch. Dana wasn't the only staff member pretty fed up with him. Laura didn't like his manner at all, and Delilah just stayed away. Only Dave didn't seem to notice.

Anyway, during those lunch hours, Slater and Dr. Dave were locked in argument. It was not that they couldn't agree what to do. Neither of them knew what to do. Their concerns were more abstract. Dr. Dave wanted to find reasons for his feelings. It would have relieved him to know, for instance, that steak, cheese, and coffee were biochemical poisons that were deepening his anxiety. Slater had never seen anything, heard anything, or felt anything. Slater had no receptors, only transmitters. He wanted to shout and drive and drink and blow his trumpet. He was marvelously contemptuous of every thread Dr. Dave wanted to look at. What good had it done him, all these years, Slater declared, to pick up one tool at a time? Income, Dr. Dave said, look at my income, look at what people think of me. People, said Slater, think nothing of you. You are just a dentist, another white coat, another small thing. Every day you sit at your stool fashioning things in people's mouths, and then they close their mouths and stand up, and more than anything they want to forget you, and your work never sees the light of day.

But you, Dr. Dave said, you know nothing, you stumble through your life without a first notion, pressing yourself and your breath and your music into the world. What good has it done you, Slater, to consume without thought and express without consideration? No good, said Slater. No good. But I know that it does me no good, and you don't even know that.

And then I sit with my head against the wall, waiting for the next patient, and I can hardly move or breathe, and when the tears begin rolling down my cheeks, I just turn my head toward the window, I don't even wonder why they have come or how I might dismiss them. I hear Dana's step pause beside the door, the step of her $120 Italian high heels, for she is very particular about elegant shoes. I can imagine the flash of her curious blue eyes, but she says nothing, and when Delilah speaks from the other office, she turns and goes out, and both Slater and Dr. Dave feel gaspingly sorry for themselves. There is nothing meditative about it.

This went on until about Thursday. On Thursday, everyone in the family woke up at a quarter to nine from a sleep that could have been drug- or enchantment-induced. There was no possible consideration of anything except clothing, breakfast, and the fact that the girls were already late for school. Even Lizzie was so somnolent that she gave no thought to the embarrassment of walking into the classroom late. She lifted her arms to receive her sleeves and opened her mouth to receive her Cheerios, and Stephanie wandered around the bathroom as if she didn't know what she was doing there, and Leah let Dana dress her without a word of protest. Dana kept making toast. I kept eating it. It was buttery and delicious. She wouldn't let us hurry. She called the office and said I was busy and would be an hour and a half late, then she called the school and said that the girls would be there in time for recess. She was sleepy, too, and wandered from bathroom to bedroom half-dressed, looking for articles of clothing that were right under her nose. At ten thirty we took Leah early to day care and went to the office together, where Dana worked on the patients I had stood up. I don't think I thought of Slater or the Other or the crisis of my marriage until well into the second patient, and then the patient's malocclusion seemed more immediate, and, even, more interesting. Delilah had brought daffodils from her garden and set them on Dave's desk, and so the day had a refrain, "Aren't those lovely flowers!"

When I used to work construction, my boss would tell me about the seventeen-inch rule. The seventeen-inch rule has to do with the construction of staircases. If you add together the width of the tread and the height of the riser, they should come out to seventeen inches. If they do, the step will meet the foot. If they don't, the foot will stumble. Sometimes, if he had a remodeling job in an old house, I would check out the seventeen-inch rule, and it was always true. The effort of steps that were too steep or too shallow was always perceived by the knees and the tendons, if not by the brain. And so I would say that we had a seventeen-inch day. Patients came on time and opened calmly. Teeth nearly drilled themselves, or jumped out into my hand. Dana and Delilah chattered and murmured in the next office. Laura and Dave teased each other. At lunch, Dana and I found ourselves on the back step of the office, facing the alley, eating peanut-butter sandwiches with raspberry jam and drinking milk. Our shoulders touched. She said, "You know, I think Leah told her first joke today."

"What was that?"

"Well, she was making claws with her hands, and roaring, the way she does, and I said, 'What's the name of your monster?' and she looked at me and said, 'Diarrhea.' And then she grinned."

We laughed and our shoulders bumped.

"Do you want the last bite of this?" She held out a piece of her sandwich.

I nodded and opened my mouth. She put it in. I chewed it. We got up and went inside. An hour and a half later I was finished for the day and half expected to be met by Slater on the steps of the office, but the coast was clear. I took out my list of errands and purchases and walked toward downtown. Everything was on sale, including a very nice blue-and-green plaid Viyella shirt, 16-35, $16 marked down from $50. I put it on in the store, something I never do. As a rule I let new clothes sit in the closet for weeks before wearing them. I kept walking, looking at yards and houses and daffodils and crocuses, and felt that spurious permanency that comes with the sense of true peace. For dinner I bought boned chicken breasts and frozen pesto sauce. Dana came home and made fresh noodles.

Leah sat between Stephanie and Lizzie on the couch and they played this game: Lizzie would take Leah's face between her two palms and say, "Say yes, Leah," and then she would nod Leah's face up and down. Then Stephanie would take Leah's face from the other side and say, "Say no, Leah," and turn her head gently from side to side. None of the three could stop laughing, the two older girls from the sight of it, and from the feeling of their own power, and Leah, perhaps, from the pleasure of their attention, or perhaps from the rattling perspective shifts she experienced as they manipulated her head. I said, "Careful of her neck." But they were, without my saying anything. I pretended not to be watching them, but really I was transfixed by the passing of that baby head from hand to hand, by the way Lizzie's and Stephanie's fingers spread and flexed, by how strong their hands were with all their childish pudginess, and by how unconscious they were and yet how sensitive. I went into the kitchen. When I came back a few minutes later, the big girls were at their pictures and Leah was coloring her fingernails with a blue marker. I opened my mouth to remind her not to write on her skin, but before the first word was out, she had drawn a line from her ankle to her diaper. She looked up at me. I said, "That's naughty. Don't write on yourself." She knew I would say it, and I did. She refrained from writing on herself then as a formality until I left the room.

These are the trivia of family life, what the children do

and say, how the fragrance of dinner wafts through the house, a view of the yard through the glass of the front door, the border collie across the street barking at the UPS man, a neighbor who has been hardly noticed these last weeks bringing the packets of seed you ordered together, looking at you quizzically and with concern, then turning away, making a joke upon herself. One by one they come upon the senses, charge along the neurons, leap the synapses, electrify the brain, and there is a moment, a moment of a specific duration which I don't remember, before the synapses jam, when the ear hears, the nose smells, the eyes see, the fingers sense the cool smooth foil of the seed packets.

We ate dinner.

We watched "Family Ties," then "Cheers." We put the children to bed and watched "Hill Street Blues."

Dana was sitting beside me on the couch. She yawned and turned toward me. I saw my face in the pupils of her eyes, then I saw that she was smiling. She said, "I can't believe I'm so tired. Are you going to sit up?"

I was, and I did, alone in the silent living room, with the lights off and a beer warming in my hand. It seemed to me that the unexpected peace of the day had left me dizzy with pleasure, such pleasure that its prospective loss made my stomach queasy. Feelings are in the body as well as in the mind, is what he said. I lay back on the carpet, on the floor of the organ that was my house, and felt my family floating above me, suspended only by two-by-fours as narrow as capillaries and membranes of flooring. My pulse beat in my ears and the walls of the house seemed to throb with it. I closed my eyes and took some deep breaths. From China, from California, state by state, patient by patient, the flu had arrived.

I wonder if it is possible to prepare yourself for anything. Of course I lay there, saying, This is the flu, it isn't supposed to last more than two or three days, I should find the Tylenol. In the moment I didn't feel bad, really, a little queasy, a degree feverish. The disease wasn't a mystery to me. I know what a virus looks like, how it works. I could imagine the invasion and the resistance. In fact, imagining the invasion and the resistance took my attention off the queasiness and the feverishness. But when I opened my eyes and my gaze fell upon the bookcases looming above me in the half-light, I shuddered reflexively, because the books seemed to swell outward from the wall and threaten to drop on me, and my thoughts about the next few days had exactly that quality as well. I did not see how we would endure, how I would endure.

There are many moments in every marriage that are so alike that they seem to be the same moment, appearing and vanishing, giving the illusion of time passing, and of no time passing, giving the illusion that a marriage is a thing everlasting. One of these recurring moments, for Dana and me, has always had to do with getting ready—finding a clear position to take up before the avalanche of events, like semester exams, births, vacations. Perhaps we practiced for this every night that we coasted down Cloud Street on my bike. That hill was not only long, it curved sharply to the right and had three steep dips. I suppose, looking back, that the precipice, such as it was, lasted seven or eight blocks before flattening out. Dana's apartment was about a block and a half from the top of the hill, and the first night I took her out I was so exhilarated that I put my feet on the handlebars of my bike and coasted all the way to the stoplight, eleven blocks from Dana's house.

The next time we went out, I suggested that we coast

down it together. I remember the way that her eyelids snapped
open at the idea and her stare locked into mine, but it took
her only a second to say yes, and then we had to do it. I
said, "Sit on the handlebars, then," and she did. She put her
hands in front of mine, balanced with the small of her back,
and looked straight ahead, straight at the first dip, and I
thought, We are going to die now. I settled the bones of my
ass on the seat and tightened my fingers on the grips. I pushed
off and pedaled. I did not want to drift into it, whatever it
was, I wanted to pump into it. It was agony. The bike was
surprisingly front-heavy. I could hardly manage the dips, and
skidded dangerously to the left when the right-hand curve
came up. Our weight carried us a block past the stoplight,
which, fortunately, was green.

After we had stopped, we didn't even speak about it,
but resumed our conversation about dental matters while
walking the thirteen blocks back up the hill. This time we
didn't stop at Dana's house, but climbed to the top, where
I stood holding the bike while she hoisted herself on. Looking
back, it is that moment I remember, that recurring moment,
always the same, of her hands and her thighs and her back,
their stillness, the lifting of my foot onto the right pedal.
Taking a clear position. I wonder why she trusted me so. I
do not discount the possibility of simple stupidity.

Now, the flu. Three steep dips and a sharp curve to the
right. People without children don't begin to know the test
that these illnesses present. But there was no clear position
to be taken, and no one to take it with. I lay on the floor
until about three, when I went upstairs and puked into the
toilet. Then I lay in the hallway outside the bathroom, shivering with fever and waiting to puke again. At six, Dana
found me, gazed down with a knowing look, and went to

find the seltzer, the Tylenol, the thermometer, the cool wash-cloth, my pajamas, a pillow so that I could remain in the hallway, where I found a kind of solitary and rigorous comfort. The children thought it was very peculiar and amusing to step over me. I was too dizzy to care.

They abandoned me. The children went to school and day care without a backward look; Dana went early to the office to take care of my patients, with only a shout from the front door that she was leaving now, would I be all right? I got my own juice, my own blanket, drew my own bath, because it seemed as if that would ease the aches and pains. I did everything for myself, because they were all off, doing as they pleased, healthy and happy. I could see out the window that it was a beautiful day, and I imagined them all dazed by the sparkle of the light, on the street, on the playground, all thoughts of me blasted out of them. Lizzie would be working in her reading workbook, Stephanie drawing pictures of the family, Leah making turtles out of egg cartons and poster paints, Dana mixing up amalgam on her tray, all of them intent only on their work, no matter how much I might think of them. Just then the phone rang, and it was Dave. He said, "Dana wanted me to call and ask if you needed anything." I said, "No. I just took some Tylenol." After that I got into the bathtub and floated there for an hour, resenting the fact that I had left my juice next to the telephone in the bedroom. Drying myself, I was dizzy again and nearly fell down. I entertained myself with thoughts of hitting my head on the bathtub and suffering a subdural hematoma; then I staggered into the bedroom and fell across the bed, already mostly asleep. Three hours later, I resurrected. I was clear-eyed, cool, happy. The forces of resistance had won an early victory.

Lizzie threw up for the first time while she was watching "The Flintstones" and eating her Hershey bar. She made it to the front hallway, but not to the bathroom. Stephanie was not sympathetic. Leah, carrying her Play Family garage from the living room to the kitchen, could not be prevented from stepping in it. Lizzie had already fled upstairs, Stephanie was hiding her nose in the sofa cushions, and Leah's wet bare footprint followed her into the dining room. I went for paper towels and a bucket, and I heard Lizzie, panicky, shouting from upstairs, "Daddy! Daddy!" She stumbled from somewhere above my head to somewhere else, and began to retch again. Just then, mop in one hand and bucket in the other, I felt all the grief of the last weeks drain away, to be replaced, not by panic, but by order. I caught Leah, wiped her foot off, and spread some paper towels over the mess in the hall. Then I went to Lizzie, who was draped over the toilet, and carried her into her bedroom, where I laid her on her bed, undid her clothes, and surrounded her with towels. Her face was red and soaked with tears, and I thought, I can't help you. I wiped her face with a cool washcloth, and then Stephanie shouted from downstairs, "She's going to get in it! She's getting near it! Daddy! Daddy!"

Lizzie said, "Don't go away."

That was the beginning.

What is it possible to give? Last fall I was driving to the office in a downpour, and I saw a very fat woman cross the street in front of the bus depot and stick out her thumb. No raincoat, no umbrella. I stopped and let her in. The office was about three blocks down, but I thought I would drive her wherever she needed to go in town. She said she was going to Kinney, a town about ten miles east, and it occurred to me simply to drive her there. She was wearing cloth shoes and carrying all her belongings in a terry-cloth bag. I don't think I answered, but she spoke anyway. She said, "My husband works out there. I just got in from California, after two months, and the whole time he was sending me these postcards, saying, Come back, come back, and so I bought my ticket." She fell silent. Then she looked at me and said, "Well, I called him up to say I'd got my ticket, and he said right there, 'Well, I want a divorce, anyway.' So here I am. He works out there."

I said, "Maybe you can change his mind."

"I hope so. She works out there where he works, too. I want to get to them before they get into work. If I can't change his mind, I'm going to beat him up right there in the parking lot." She looked at me defiantly.

I said, "Why don't I drop you at the Amoco station at the corner of Front Street? You can stand under the awning, and there ought to be a lot of people turning toward Kinney there."

"Yeah."

After I got to the office, I thought maybe I could have bought her an umbrella, but I didn't go out and get her one, did I? It perplexes me, what it is possible to give a stranger, what it is possible to give a loved one, the difference between desire and need, how it is possible to divine what is helpful. I might say that I would give Dana anything to ensure her presence in our house, our office, our family, but in saying this I have only traded the joy of giving for the despair of payment. I went downstairs and cleaned up the mess, then I went back upstairs and wiped Lizzie's face again with a newly wrung-out washcloth. If you stimulate the nerve endings in a pleasurable way, the neurons are less capable of carrying pain messages to the brain, and the brain is fooled. Dana was an hour late from work.

I should say that Lizzie heaved twelve times in four hours, so much that we were forcing ginger ale down her throat so that something, anything, could come back up. And she was fighting every drop, and screaming in panic, and throwing herself back and forth among the towels on her bed. We didn't have dinner, of course, but we did laundry, all the nightgowns, all the sheets, all the towels. About eleven, Dana said, "You're better," as if she had just noticed.

"Thirteen hours, normal to normal in thirteen hours."

"That's something, anyway."

"Not a basis for confidence, though."

She pursed her lips. "I wish you weren't always so pessimistic."

"As long as this lasts, why don't we avoid talking about how we always are?"

"Okay, but no sarcasm, either."

"A deal." We shook hands. Lizzie threw up four more times before morning, then six times on Saturday. When I called the pediatrician for a little reassurance and told him she had thrown up twenty-two times, he said, "That's impossible."

Dana says that they are formed at birth, and that they spend their whole childhoods simply revealing themselves. With a sort of arrogance that you might say is typical of her, she says that she knew all this in advance, as soon as she laid her mother's hands on them, that Lizzie did not care to snuggle, that Stephanie's neonatal thoughts were elsewhere, that Leah wanted to melt into the warmth of Dana's flesh. Some people cannot, will not be comforted. Lizzie is this way. She tosses off the covers and complains of the cold. Her joints ache, and she won't take the medicine. A swallow of seltzer gives her mouth such cool pleasure that she won't take another. She writhed about among the towels, needing and fighting sleep, and I sat near her, sometimes smoothing her forehead with the wrung-out washcloth and contemplating her doom in much the same way that you contemplate their future glory when they do well in school or learn to read at three and a half. Then she fell asleep about ten and slept all night, not doomed, but saved one more time.

Dana lay next to me in a snore, and I thought of the soul, nacreous protoplasm, ringed in the iron of the self, weak little translucent hands on the bars, pushing, yanking, desperate for release. The moonlight stood flat in the window glass, as if caught there, and I turned and pressed myself against the warmth of my disappearing wife. Leah awakened at four. She would consent to be held only by me, and there was no sitting down allowed, only walking. A torture, in the middle of the night, that could have been devised by the KGB.

That was Sunday, the resurrection of Lizzie and the marathon of Leah, kitchen, dining room, living room, an endless circle. Sometimes Dana handed me food and drink, as in the old Kingston Trio song about the fellow who got stuck on the MTA. Dana kept putting on records, to keep me occupied, and sometimes she took Leah from me, but the screams were unrelenting. Sometimes I put her down in her bed, when she seemed to be asleep, but she always woke up and called out for me. Sometimes I staggered under the weight. Sometimes I got so dizzy from the circling that I nearly fell down. I had a chant: Normal to normal in thirteen hours. Maybe it was a prayer.

For dinner Lizzie and Stephanie wanted pizza. I circled. Leah's head rested back on her neck against my shoulder. Her mouth was open and her eyes were closed. One arm was tossed around my neck and her fingers hung in the collar of my shirt. From time to time I sat down in the rocking chair (this was always accompanied by a groan of protest from Leah) and rocked until the protests grew unbearable. The pizza came and Lizzie didn't want any. Stephanie ate only a single piece, because Lizzie pointed out to her that mushrooms had been put on by mistake. Dana screamed at them, threw away all the rest of the pizza, said we would never order another one, and sent them to their rooms; then she flopped on the couch, ashamed and unhappy, and followed me with her gaze while I circled the downstairs.

She said, "You're such a hero. I can't believe it."

"What else is there to do?"

"Yes, but you don't even seem to want to strangle every one of them. I do. Put us all out of our misery."

I headed for the kitchen and returned. "Are you miserable?"

Her eyes lifted to mine. She said, "I expect to be." I stopped walking and looked at her, then started again. She looked away and shrugged. "The flu always hits me like a ton of bricks."

"I didn't have it too badly. Maybe this one is worse for children than adults."

"But you never really get sick. I always think there's a kind of purity about you. Untouched. You remind me of some kind of flower."

"A flower?"

"I don't mean that you aren't masculine. You know that. I don't know." She looked out the window, speculating.

"You know when you lean down and look right into a tulip? You know the way the petals look thick with color, but thin with light, permanent and delicate at the same time?"

"I suppose."

"That makes me think of you. Always has."

"Do you think of me?"

She looked back at me. She smiled slightly and said, "I have been lately, for some reason."

"Dana—"

"I better go and release them from bondage, or they'll be furious for the rest of the night." And then the whirlwind swept us up again.

However the flu took Leah, with nausea she couldn't puke out or give voice to, with aches and pains, with lethargy, it took her for three days, and I walked her for most of those three days. At first I was tired and bored: she was heavy, and the urge to put her off was more pressing than hunger, more like a raging thirst. I would panic at the thought of the hours, even the minutes, before me, of walking and carrying until my whole left side, the side she leaned upon, was numb, and my legs were leaden. After a while, though, say late Sunday night, it was as if Leah and our joining had sunk more deeply into me, so that I only did it, didn't think about it, didn't rebel against it. They say that this happens with the KGB, too.

Dana had gone to bed, leaving one lamp in the living room dimly lit. I remember looking at my watch, at the way the time looked there, eleven fifteen, and the previous four weeks of nights, myself lying awake in fear or hope or whirring thought, suddenly seemed like a deck of shuffling cards to me, and yet each moment had been a lengthy agony. That was why the face of my watch was so familiar to me—I had looked at it repeatedly in disbelief at the tormented slowness of time. Then I remember looking down at Leah, whose face, as familiar as the face of my watch, glowed with fever and sleep. Her mouth was partly open and she breathed at me. I felt the tiny rush of it on my lips, where the nerves cluster, on my cheeks, like the first breeze after you have shaved your beard, even on my forehead. There was a fragrance to it, too, sour and pungent, the odor of sick child, but so familiar, so entwined with the lasting pleasure of holding the child's flesh to your own, that I drank it in. I lifted her higher and kissed her hot cheek, hot silk against the searching ganglia. I shifted her over to the right and she settled in. It seemed to me that I had never loved anything—object, or feeling, or person— the way I loved her right now. Love is in the body as well as the mind, a rush of blood to the surface, maybe, an infinitesimal yearning stretch of the nerve endings. I looked at her without seeing her, blinded by the loveliness of her nose, the grace of her forehead, the curl of her upper lip and the roundness of the lower. I will never see her, hard as I try to look past love. My eyes will always cast a light over her, and I will always think that this love, mine for her, is a dear thing. But it is as common as sand, as common as flesh.

After all, it was harder to cherish hers for me. Hard to appreciate the way she climbed the stairs looking for me, held my leg when I was trying to walk across the kitchen, yearned for my presence in the middle of the night, hard even to appreciate her glances into my face, her man-pleasing chatter, the stroke of her baby fingers on my forehead. And these hours of walking were unbearable, although I was bearing them. I stopped and looked down at her, thinking, Open your eyes. After a long while, she opened her eyes with a sigh, and I said, "Leah, it's time for bed."

She said, "Not go to bed."

"Yes, I'm tired. I'll walk you in the morning."

"Picky up."

"I'm going to take you to your bed now. You can have a bottle of juice. Tonight, even the dentist says you can have a bottle of juice."

"Picky up."

I carried her into the kitchen, filled a bottle with diluted juice, and began up the stairs.

"No bed."

"Time for bed. I'll lie down beside you on the floor."

"No bed."

I put her in. She was wide awake. I lay on the rug, and she rolled over and looked down at me through the bars. Her eyes were big in the dark. She reached her hand through the bars, and I gave her mine, though it was awkward. She looked at me and held my hand, and I fell asleep. Maybe she never fell asleep. We were up and walking by six. When Dana got up, I said, "I talked her into letting me get some sleep. I talked her into it." Dana handed me a piece of toast. I grew, once again, overconfident. The goodness of warm toast, the sweetness of cold orange juice, the attentions of my wife, the new maturity of my two-year-old. "Two years old!" I said. "I *talked* her into it." I thought I knew what I was doing.

We walked all of that day, until about six, when she got down out of my arms to interfere with Lizzie and Stephanie at their Parcheesi game. After dinner her fever went up and we walked until eleven. On Tuesday, we walked from six fifteen in the morning until ten thirty, when she got down for good at the sight of the Barbie bubbling spa boxed up in the front hall closet. I set it up. I found every Barbie and every water toy in the house, all the hair ornaments and four spoons. I gave her Tylenol and a bottle of juice, and then I went into the living room and collapsed on the couch. After a few minutes I could hear her start talking to herself and humming. I ached from the soles of my feet to my chin.

At noon I still hadn't moved, and Leah came in the living room to chat. She said, "Are you sleeping now?"

I said, "You're soaking wet."

She said, "Are you sleeping on the couch?"

I said, "Let's go upstairs and change out of your pajamas. Is your diaper wet?" And just then Dana walked in, her face as white as her jacket, which she hadn't bothered to take off. She closed the door behind her and, without speaking, turned and climbed the stairs. I said, "What's the main symptom?" and she said, "Aches and pains. My joints feel as if they're fracturing and knitting every second." Her voice trailed off and I sat up on the couch. Leah said, "Are you waking up now?"

Stephanie and Lizzie came in at three ten, when I was thinking about dinner. I hadn't thought about dinner in four days, and I was ruminating over steak and baked potatoes and green beans in cheese sauce, my father's favorite meal. They threw down their backpacks and called for milk. While I was in the kitchen, someone turned on the TV. By the time I had returned, Stephanie was face down on the couch. I was nearly jovial. I thought I knew what I was doing. I said, "Is it your turn, Steph? Have you got it?"

She rolled over. She said, "I feel bad now."

"Do you want to go upstairs? Mommy's up there. She's got it, too, but I have a feeling it will go away fast for you and Mommy." She held out her arms and I picked her up. There was Tylenol in every room in the house, and I grabbed some. She said, "Ooooh." It was a long-drawn-out and deeply resigned moan, the sound, it later turned out, of the fever rising in her veins like steam in a radiator. By the time I had carried her to her room, my shirt where she lay against me was soaked with her sweat. She said, "The yellow one."

I thought she was asking for a certain nightgown. I said, "Sweetie, you don't have a yellow one. How about the pink one?"

"Throw away the yellow one. My house."

I sat her on the bed and counted out five children's Tylenol. She collapsed, and I sat her up, opened her mouth with that practiced dental firmness, and put in the tablets, one by one. Her hair was soaked with sweat. She said, "Melon. Melon, melon, melon." I laid her out, and put my hand across her forehead. She was incandescent. I took my hand away and placed it in my lap. From downstairs came the sound of the Superfriends. From down the hall came Dana's voice, low and annoyed, saying, "Shit. Oh shit." She is not long-suffering in illness, and generally keeps up a steady stream of expletives as long as she feels bad. I sat quietly, because in myself I felt panic, a little void, needle-thin but opening. The thermometer was on the table next to Lizzie's bed. I stared at it for a long time, then at Stephanie, then at my hand reaching for it, then at my hand putting it in her mouth. The Superfriends broke for a commercial, Lizzie called, "Daddy!" Dana said, "Damn I hate this," and the thermometer, held up to the light, read 104.2.

There is the permanent threat of death. In the fifties, people used to grow trees through the roofs of their houses sometimes, and I often think of death as an invisible tree planted in our living room. When the doors are closed and locked, the insurance paid, the windows shaded, injury and the world excluded so that we, thinking that we know what we are doing, can sit complacently at the dining room table, that invisible tree rustles, flourishes, adds a ring of girth. Any flight of stairs is treacherous, the gas furnace is a bomb waiting to go off, Renuzit may stray, unaided by the human hand, from top shelf to bottom. A child carrying a scissors might as well be holding a knife to her breast; bicycles beside the door yearn to rush into traffic. A tongue of flame can lick out of the wall socket, up a cord carelessly left plugged in, and find the folds of a curtain. From time to time, unable to sleep, I have lain in bed counting household hazards: radon in the basement, petroleum products in the carpeting, gas fumes in the stove. I don't often think of illness, but a child in the next block had meningitis last year. When Eileen, that is the mother, went to the hospital, they looked her in the face and said, "Twenty-five percent chance of death, twenty-five percent chance of severe brain damage, twenty-five percent chance of minimal brain damage, twenty-five percent chance of full recovery," and they were so matter-of-fact, Eileen says, that she just nodded and said, "Oh. Thanks," as if she were taking a rain check on a sale at K-mart.

I wonder once in a while how my father would have reacted if one of us had died. It seems to me that he would have noticed something missing, that my absence, or my brother's, would have prickled at him through the day, and he would have upheld the forms of grief, but I don't know that he ever really looked at us, or perceived enough about us so that the removal of one of us would have been a ripping of flesh. Soon enough he would have gotten behind the stove or the clothes dryer or the dehumidifier with his electrical meter and forgotten about it entirely, as he did about us alive. Dana said that I often underestimate him, but in this case, I think he was a wise man, to have addressed himself to the world at large like that, to have stood in front of us, only half perceiving us, reassured by the shuffle of our feet and our sighings and breathings that all of us, whoever we were, were back there.

When you are in the habit of staring at your children, as almost everyone my age that I know is, of talking about them, analyzing them, touching them, bathing them, putting them to bed, when you have witnessed their births and followed, with anxious eyes, the rush of the doctor and nurses out of the delivery room to some unknown machine room where some unknown procedure will relieve some unknown condition, when you have inspected their stools and lamented their diaper rash and, mostly, held their flesh against yours, there is no turning away. Their images are imprinted too variously and plentifully on your brain, and they are with you always. When I agreed with Dana that I wanted to be "an involved father," I foresaw the commitment of time. I didn't foresee the commitment of risk, the commitment of the heart. I didn't foresee how a number on a thermometer would present me with, paralyze me with, every evil possibility. Stephanie lay there, stupefied with fever. Lizzie came into the room. She said, "Didn't you hear me? I want some more milk." She sounded annoyed.

"You can pour it yourself."

"I can't. It's too heavy."

"Don't talk to me in that tone of voice. Can't you say please?"

"Please!"

"Say it as if you mean it."

She drew it out. "Pleeeeease."

"I'll be down in a minute."

"It's always in a minute. That's what you and Mommy always say—in a minute. Then you forget."

"You aren't the only person in the house, Elizabeth."

"You always say that, too." She backed away, not sure how far she could take this discussion. She glanced at Stephanie on the bed. I said, "Stephanie has a very high fever."

"Is it dangerous?"

I turned the word over in my mind, because it is a big word in the family vocabulary, a dangerous word, in fact, that always signals to Lizzie that she ought to panic. I was still rather annoyed about her recent demanding tone. I contemplated sobering her up, but I needed her as my ally, didn't I? I said, "It's not good, but it's not dangerous." She nodded. I said, "Do me a favor, and go ask Mommy how she feels." She turned in the doorway and called, "Mommy! How do you feel?" Dana groaned. I surveyed Lizzie and wondered, Is this defiance on her part, ill-taught manners, stupidity? I said, "Go ask her. Be polite. I need you to help me." Now she surveyed me. I was not kidding. She went into the master bedroom, and I stuck the thermometer back in Stephanie's mouth, thinking that the Tylenol would have had time to take effect. 104.1. Lizzie returned. "She feels as if she's been run over."

"What's Leah doing?"

"Watching TV."

"Can you do everything I say for the next two days?"

"Do you mean like cleaning my room?"

"I mean like getting me stuff and watching Leah, and getting stuff for Mommy."

She shrugged.

"I think you can. It's important."

"Okay." She and I looked at each other. Her eyes are blue, too, but darker blue than Dana's, more doubtful. Simultaneously I thought that this would be a good lesson in responsibility for her and that no lessons, however good, would preserve her from her own nature. I said, "Go into the bathroom and get a washcloth and wring it out in cold water. I'm going to talk to Mommy for a minute, and then we are going to try and cool Stephie off, okay?"

Dana lay on her side with her eyes closed. The lids were purple all the way to her eyebrows, as if she had eyeshadow on, but the skin of her face was opaquely pale. The blood was elsewhere, heart, brain. She was not sleeping, but I don't think she was aware of me. Her lips formed words, Fuck this, I can't take this, dammit. I leaned down and said, "Can I get you anything?"

Her eyes opened. She uttered, "Did you have these aches and pains?"

"Not really."

"I've never felt anything like it. It must be what rheumatoid arthritis is like."

"Anything else?"

"A little woozy. How's Stephanie?"

"Temperature."

"How much?"

"Lots."

She looked at me for a long moment. "How much?"

"104."

"Did you call Danny?"

"He'll just say bring her in at 105. I gave her some Tylenol and I'm going to give her a lukewarm bath."

"Oh." Her voice was very low. She closed her eyes.

After a moment, tears began to run through the lashes, over the bridge of her nose, onto the pillowcase.

"She'll be all right."

She nodded, without opening her eyes.

"What's wrong?"

"I'm sad for us."

"We've had the flu before."

"I'm sad for us, anyway." She snorted and wiped her face on the quilt.

"We'll be all right, too." She opened her eyes and looked at me, sober, speculative, in retreat. Not if she can help it, I thought. I said, "I love you."

"I know." But though she continued to look at me, she didn't reciprocate.

Finally I said, "Well. I'm going to work on Stephie." She nodded.

Lizzie was doing a good job. Stephanie lay on her back, with her eyes closed and her chin slightly raised. Lizzie was smoothing the washcloth over her forehead and down her cheeks. She had a look of concentration on her face, the same look she gets when she is writing something. I stood quietly in the doorway watching them and listening to Leah mount the stairs. Soon she came into view, her hand reaching up to grasp the banister, her eyes on her feet, careful. She looked up and smiled. I would like to have all these moments again.

Just then, Stephanie threw out her arm, smacking Lizzie in the face. Lizzie jumped back in surprise, already crying, and I was upon them with reassurances. "She didn't mean it, honey. Stephie? Stephie? Are you there, sweetie? Do you want to take a little bath?" She was tossing herself around the bed. She said, "Megan, don't. Don't!" I picked her up to carry her into the bathroom and she nearly jerked out of my arms. She was soaked with sweat and slippery. After the bath, she was still above 104. It was like a floor she could not break through.

I kept a record:

6 p.m.: 104.1
6:40 p.m.: 104.2
8 p.m. (more Tylenol): 104
9 p.m.: 104.2
10:35 : 104.2
Midnight: 104.4
12:30 : 104.4
3 a.m.: 104.6 (another bath)
4 a.m.: 104.4
6 a.m.: 104.2

I longed for some magic number, either 103.8 or 105, for either reassurance or the right to take her to the hospital. She writhed and spoke and sweated and grew smaller in my eyes, as if the flesh were melting off her. I kept reminding myself that the fever is not the illness but the body fighting off the illness. It is hard to watch, hands twitch for something to do. And I was beat, after those nights with Leah, but even if I dozed, I would wake after an hour, and my first feeling was raging curiosity: what would it read this time?

8 a.m.: 104.2

Lizzie walked to school alone and I took Leah to her day care. I ran home, my fingers itching for the thermometer. I was ready to believe any magic, but none had taken effect. I gave her more Tylenol, another bath, took a shower, stepped on the scale. I had lost twelve pounds since Dana's opera. The High Stress Family Diet.

9:30 a.m.: 104.4. Dan, the pediatrician, told me to keep taking her temperature.

11 a.m.: 104.4

1 p.m.: 104.4

3 p.m.: 104.4

6 p.m.: 104.4

After I read it, I shook the thermometer, just to see if the mercury was able to register any other number. I called the pediatrician again. He said that it would go down very soon. I said, "It's not impossible that it could just stay at this level, is it?"

He said, "Anything is possible." I was glad to hear him admit it.

8 p.m.: 104.6

10 p.m.: 104.6

I should say that I talked to her the whole day. "Stephanie," I said, "this stinks, doesn't it? We've been at this for days, it seems to me. Pure torture, an endless task. Sisyphean, you might say. I remember the myth of Sisyphus quite well, actually. We read it in seventh grade. You will probably read it in seventh grade, too. I also remember the myth of Tantalus. He kept trying to bite an apple that would move out of the way when he leaned his head toward it. Sisyphus had to roll a stone up the mountain, and then watch it roll back down again. I think I remember it because that's what seventh grade seemed like to me. Anyway, sooner or later you will know all this stuff. And more. The thing is, after you know it, it will float in and out of your consciousness in a random way, so that if you ever just want to sit and talk to your own daughter like this, not having a conversation but just talking to keep her ears greased, as it were, then all of this stuff will come in handy. But I am here to tell you, Stephie dear, that every word, whatever its meaning, gets us closer to tomorrow or the next day, when you will sit up and look around, and I will breathe a long sigh of relief." The paternal patter. During the night, it eased toward 105, and I took it every forty-five minutes. At two, Dana got up to spell me, but when I got up at two thirty, I found her passed out in the hallway and carried her back to bed.

She is light. She is only 5′ 4″, though she seems taller to the patients because she always wears those three-inch Italian heels in the office. People marvel at this, but in fact she doesn't stand on her feet all day, she sits on a stool. The shoes flatter her ankles, her hips, her waist, everything up to the back of her head, because everything is connected, of course. She is thin. She weighs 107 or 108. Once I had a good grasp on her, I could have carried her anywhere. She was wearing a white flannel nightgown scattered with tiny red hearts. She was warm and damp, her hair was askew, she would have said that she didn't look her best. A silk shirt, those heels, a linen or cotton or wool skirt, a good haircut, lipstick—that is looking her best, she would have said; a fine-grained surface, a sort of enameling. Women who are more relaxed find her a little cold, or archaic, or formal, but it seems to me that she has poured herself into a sort of dental mold, too. Dentists make a lot of money. Dental conventions are full of dandies. Two dentists in conference in the lobby of the Dallas Hyatt are more likely to be talking about tailors than about inlays. Her body is not yielding. It has a lot of tensile strength that is inherited, I think. Her brother Joe can bench-press 250 pounds, though he doesn't lift weights as a hobby. In any pickup softball game, her sister Frances has amazing power at the plate. To lift Dana in one's arms is to feel not weight but elastic resistance.

To take Dana into one's arms, and to be taken into hers, is to feel, not yielding, but strength. When she holds your hand, she grips it hard. When you hug her, she hugs back. When you kiss her, her lips, which are firm, press against yours. Picking her up reminded me of those things, reminded me that retreat isn't always her mode, is rarely her mode, has never been her mode, is, in fact, a function of point of view, of where you are in the field of her activities. I pushed the covers back with my foot and laid her down. She groaned. I pulled her nightgown over her feet, pulled the sheet up to her chin, then the blanket.

Stephanie had been asleep since about eleven. I opened the curtains of her room partway, and shook down the thermometer by the streetlight outside. I opened her drawer and took out a fresh nightgown. The house was quiet, and I was fully awake somehow, though I hadn't had a full night's sleep in six days, or slept the sleep of the innocent in weeks. The darkness, when I closed the curtains, seemed a presence in the house, sensible, like heat. I let it envelop me where I sat on Stephanie's bed. I might have said that it pressed against my skin, got under my clothes, filtered into my hair, coal dust, blackness itself, sadness. I reached out my hand and put it on Stephanie's small hip under the covers. It submerged her, too, pressed her down against the dark pillow so that I could barely see her face. Even her blond hair, coiled against her neck, moist with sweat, gave off no light. Now the darkness felt as though it were getting into me—by osmosis through the skin, mingled with my inhalations, streaming into my eyes and up the optic nerves to seep among the coils of the brain, replacing meditation. It pooled in my ears. My pulmonary arteries carried blood into my lungs, where it was enriched with darkness, not oxygen, and then it spread through the circulatory system, to toes and fingertips and scalp. The marrow of my bones turned black, began spawning black blood cells. And so thought was driven out at last. Meditation, the weighing of one thing against another, the dim light of reflection, the labor of separating thread from thread, all gone.

I ran my hand gently up Stephanie's back and jostled her shoulder. "Time, sweetie," I said. "I need to take your temperature." I jostled her again. No response. Now I put the thermometer on the night table and lifted her in my arms. Her head flopped back against my shoulder, and I put the thermometer into her partly open mouth, then held her jaws closed. I was glad she seemed to be getting sounder sleep—she had been restless for two nights now. I counted slowly to 250, then took out the thermometer and laid it gently on the night table. Then I unbuttoned her nightgown and slid her out of it. Her skin was so damp that it was hard to get the sleeves of the clean one up her arms. I stretched her out on the mattress, smoothed the blanket over her. Then I carried the thermometer into the bathroom and turned on the light. 105.2. My hand was still on the switch. I pushed it down and submerged myself in darkness again.

I did not have a thought, but I had a vision, or an image, a fleeting memory of the stars as they looked the night I drove out on the interstate, as many stars as worlds as eras as species as humans as children, an image of the smallness of this one gigantic child with her enormous fever. When each of them was born, Dana used to say, "There's one born every minute," but she was grinning, ecstatic with the importance of it. "Isn't it marvelous what you can do with a little RNA?" she would say, just to diminish them a little. But they couldn't be diminished. So, however many worlds and species and children there were and had been, I was scared to death. I crept to the phone and called the clinic, where, thank God, they were wide-awake. I said, "Is it possible to die of the flu?" They put a nurse on right away. Was she very sick?

"What does that mean? She has a temperature of 105.2."

"But how is she acting?"

"She's not acting any way. She's asleep."

"Is she dehydrated?"

"She urinated at around ten thirty. We've maintained lots of fluids."

"Is she hallucinating?"

"She's asleep."

"Is she lethargic?"

"She's *asleep*, goddammit!"

"Is it possible to wake her?" Her voice was patient and slow. Now I had another image, the image of Stephanie's head flopping back on my shoulder and the utter unconsciousness of her state. I said, "I'll try." She said, "I'll hold."

And then I went in and I sat her up and I shook her and shook her, and I said, "Stephanie! Stephanie! Wake up! Wake up! Stephanie? Listen to me. I want you to wake up!" She groaned, writhed, protested. She was hard to wake up. I reported this to the nurse and she left the phone for the obligatory hold. After a while she came back and told me to bring her in. Her tone was light enough, as if it were three in the afternoon rather than three in the morning. I began to cry. I began to cry that my wife was unconscious with the flu, too, and that I didn't dare leave the other children in her care, and pretty soon the doctor came on, and it wasn't Dan but Nick, someone whom we know slightly, in a professional way, and he said, "Dave? Is that you, Dave?" and I of course was embarrassed, and then the light went on and there was Dana, blinking but upright in the doorway, and she said, "What is going on?" and I handed her the phone, and Nick told her what I had told the nurse, and I went into Stephanie's bedroom and began to wrap her in blankets so that I could take her to the hospital, and I knew that the next morning, when Stephanie's fever would have broken, I would be extremely divorced from and a little ashamed of my reactions, and it was true that I was. They sent us home from the hospital about noon. Dana was making toast at the kitchen table, Leah was running around in her pajama top without a diaper, and Lizzie had escaped to school.

I sat Stephanie at the table, and she held out her wrist bracelet. They had spelled her name wrong, *Stefanie Herst.*

"That's the German way," said Dana. "It's pronounced 'Stefania.' Shall we call you that now?"

Stephanie laughed and said, "Can I have that one?" pointing at the toast Dana was buttering, and Dana handed it to her, and she folded it in two and shoved it into her mouth, and Dana buttered her another one. They were weak but in high spirits, the natural effect of convalescence. I went into the living room and lay down on the couch. I looked at my watch. It read 12:25. After a moment I looked again. It read 5:12. It was not wrong. Across the room on the TV, Maria and Gordon and some child were doing "long, longer, and longest." Leah was watching them, Lizzie was erasing and redoing her papers from school, and Stephanie was coloring. Dana appeared in the doorway, wiping her hands on a towel, then smiled and said, "You're awake."

"I'm resurrected. Are you sure I was breathing all this time?"

"We had a nice day."

"How do you feel?"

"Back to normal."

"How normal?"

"I'm making fried chicken."

"Mashed potatoes?"

"Cream gravy, green beans with browned almonds, romaine lettuce."

"The Joe McManus blue-plate special."

"I set a place for him at the table, just like Elijah."

The ironic middle. We were married again, and grinning. We've always made a lot of good jokes together. I heaved myself off the couch and went to the shower. Not so long ago, Lizzie came home and said. "You know when you let the bathwater out and there's a lot of little gray stuff in it?"

I said, "Yeah."

She said, "That's your skin."

I stood in the shower for about twenty minutes.

And then it was Friday, everyone in school, day care, work, all support services functioning, the routine as smooth as stainless steel. I was thirty-five, which is young these days, resilient, vital, glad to be in the office, glad to see Laura and Dave, glad to drill and fill and hold X-rays up to the light. In our week away, the spring had advanced, and the trees outside my examination room window were budded out.

As soon as the embryo can hear, what it hears is the music of the mother's body—the *lub-dup* of her heart, the riffle of blood surging in her arteries, the slosh of amniotic fluids. What sound, so close up, does the stomach make, the

esophagus? Do the disks of the spine creak? Do the lungs
sound like a bellows or a conch shell? Toward the end of
pregnancy when the pelvis loosens, is there a groan of protest
from the bony plates? Maybe it is such sounds that I am
recalling when I sit on my chair with the door to my office
half closed and feel that rush of pleasure hearing the conversation in the hall, or in Dana's office. Delilah's voice swells:
"And then they—" It fades. Dave: "But if you—" Dana:
"Tomorrow we had better—" The simplest words, words
without content, the body of the office surging and creaking.
Dana's heels, click click, the hydraulic hum of her dental
chair rising. In my office, I am that embryo for a second,
eyes bulging, mouth open, little hand raised, little fingers
spread. I have been so reduced by the danger of the last few
weeks that the light shines through me. Does the embryo
feel embryonic doubt and then, like me, feel himself nestling
into those sounds, that giant heart, carrying him beat by
confident beat into the future—waltz, fox-trot, march, jig,
largo, adagio, allegro? I don't sing, as Dana does, but I listen.
Jennifer Lyons, age fourteen, pushes open the door, peeps
in. "Hi," I say, "have a seat." And I am myself again, and
the workday continues.

   And continued. And continued. She made lasagna for
dinner. Saturday she got a baby-sitter and we went to the
movies. Afterward we stopped at the restaurant next to the
office and had a drink. She put her arm through mine. I
watched her face. Now I could speak, but what would I say?
If there was not this subject between us, I could have talked
about the news, our friends, the office, our daughters, but
now I could say nothing. We sat close, she put her hand on
my knee. I drank the odor of her body into the core of my
brain, where it imprinted.

On Sunday there was laundry and old food in the refrigerator. We mopped the floors, and Dana was seized with the compulsion to straighten drawers. I raked mulch off the flower beds and got out the lawn mower and climbed the ladder to clear leaves out of the eaves troughs. Lizzie and Stephanie spent the weekend obsessively exploring the neighborhood, like dogs reestablishing their territory. Leah took this opportunity to play, by herself, with every one of their toys that she had been forbidden over the winter. I liked her touch. She didn't want to damage, she only wanted to appraise. I thought of my temptation to speak on Saturday night with horror. Each of these normal weekend hours seemed like a disaster averted.

Monday at noon Dana and Delilah were late, did not appear. Dave was surprised at my surprise. Man to man. He didn't look at me. He said, looking at the floor, "Didn't you know that she canceled everything?" Man to man. I didn't look at him. I said, "Maybe she told me and I wasn't listening. It was a busy morning." Man to man. We glanced at each other briefly, embarrassed.

She was not at home at three, when I got there to wait for the big girls.

She was not at home at five fifteen, when I got back from the day-care center with Leah, or at five thirty, when I put in the baking potatoes and turned on the oven.

She was not at home at seven, when we sat down to eat our meat and potatoes. Lizzie said, "Where's Mommy?"

I said, "I don't know," and they all looked at me, even Leah. I repeated, "I don't know," and they looked at their dinners, and one by one they made up their minds to eat, anyway, and I did, too, without thinking, without prying into the mystery, without taking any position at all.

She was not at home when Leah went to bed at eight, or when Lizzie and Stephanie went to bed at nine.

She was not at home when I went to bed at eleven, or when I woke up at one and realized that she was gone. At first I considered practicalities—how we would divide up the house and the business and the odd number of children. These were dauntingly perplexing, so I considered Dana herself, the object, the force, the person that is the force within the object. In the confusion of dental school, of fighting with my father, of knowing that my draft lottery number was just on the verge of being not high enough, of taking out a lot of student loans and living on $25 a week, I remember feeling a desire for Dana when she first appeared, when she paused in the doorway that second day of class and cast her eyes about the room, that was hard and pure, that contained me and could not be contained, and I remember making that bargain that people always make—anything for this thing.

No doubt it was the same bargain that Dana was making right then, at one in the morning, somewhere else in town.

She was not at home at three, when I finally got up and went downstairs for a glass of milk, or at four, when I went back to bed and fell asleep, or at seven, when Leah started calling out, or at seven thirty, when Lizzie discovered that all the clothes she had to wear were unacceptable, or at eight forty-five, when I checked the house one last time before checking the office. Dave caught my eye involuntarily as I opened the door, and shrugged. At eleven the phone rang, and then Dave came into my examination room between patients and said, "She canceled again." I nodded and straightened the instruments on my tray. At two my last patient failed to show, and I went home to clean up for the girls.

She was sitting at the dining room table. I sat down across from her, and when she looked at me, I said, "Until last night I still thought I might be misreading the signals." She shook her head.

"Well, are you leaving or staying?"

"Staying."

"Are you sure?"

She nodded.

I said, "Let's not talk about it for a while, okay?"

She nodded. And we looked at each other. It was two thirty.

The big girls would be home in forty minutes.

Shall I say that I welcomed my wife back with great sadness, more sadness than I had felt at any other time? It seems to me that marriage is a small container, after all, barely large enough to hold some children. Two inner lives, two lifelong meditations of whatever complexity, burst out of it and out of it, cracking it, deforming it. Or maybe it is not a thing at all, nothing, something not present. I don't know, but I can't help thinking about it.

Jane Smiley was born in Los Angeles, grew up in St. Louis, and studied at Vassar and the University of Iowa, where she received her Ph.D. She now teaches at Iowa State University. She is the author of three novels, Barn Blind, At Paradise Gate, *and* Duplicate Keys, *and her stories have appeared in such magazines as* TriQuarterly, The Atlantic, *and in the Pushcart Prize anthology and the O. Henry Awards Prize Stories collection. She lives in Ames, Iowa.*

A NOTE ON THE TYPE

*The text of this book was set on the Linotron 202 in a
type face known as Garamond. The design is based on
letter forms originally created by Claude Garamond
(c. 1480–1561). Garamond was a pupil of Geoffroy
Tory and may have patterned his letter forms on Venetian
models. To this day, the type face that bears his name is
one of the most attractive used in book composition, and
the intervening years have caused it to lose little of its
freshness or beauty.*

*Composed by Crane Typesetting Service, Inc.,
Barnstable, Massachusetts*

*Printed and bound by The Haddon Craftsmen, Inc.,
Scranton, Pennsylvania*

Designed by Marysarah Quinn